TAKEN BY THE KINGPIN

EVIE ROSE

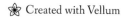

1

JEANETTE

I check the contents of my purse for the thousandth time as I walk fast—or as close to fast as my heels and floor-length dress allow. Tissues, pain killers, plasters, pocket star chart, phone.

Okay. Okay, the check makes me feel a little more in control. Ugh, I wish the Uber had turned up. But now there's none available and walking is my only option. At least the necessary pace to be less late is keeping me warm. Ish.

The London night is that cold crisp darkness, like all the warmth of the day got sucked out. I glance up, hoping for some guidance. I don't get parents, surely I should have celestial help? But there's no wisdom to be gleaned. No stars to read the future in. Just a dark woolly blanket over the city, glowing with reflected orange light.

I think sometimes my life is like a city sky. Sure, there might be a plan up there, written out in the stars. But it's obscured and muddled by all the power games I've fought against in my very-nearly twenty-one years.

I was a mafia princess. I was Sebastian Laurent's

arranged and then rejected bride. I was friends with him for an afternoon, though I no more wanted to marry him than I did my next "suitor". Aged sixteen, I was the furious and tearful one-day wife of a monster: Ross Fletcher. I was a helpless pawn in my father's power games.

Now I'm none of those things. I'm a normal girl. After years in protective custody when my marriage was discovered, but the police couldn't make the charges stick, I'm finally on the cusp of freedom. Out of school and with an admin assistant job to an astrologer and a small, boxy apartment I was allocated, reading gossip magazines showing photos of my once betrothed.

Alright, swooning over. Just a little.

But I want to prove I can be more than the feeble girl I've been brought up to be. Smarter, certainly. Not doing so well on that right now, as I should have put on ballet flats. I'm in danger of needing the emergency stash of plasters for myself.

Ouch, these shoes.

I increase my pace. No swooning. No giving up on the pretty shoes.

I arrive at the hotel panting, my breath puffs of tiny ice crystals fading into black, only a bit late. Hopefully my boss won't notice. The astrology award ceremony guests have already arrived, but Priscilla is not to know I have been rushing across the city. I might have just been lost in the crush.

I show my ticket and the attendant opens the door onto a swooping staircase down into the ballroom. Hesitating, I peer out over the crowd and butterflies take flight in my stomach. All those people, and I'm supposed to walk down the stairs and not slip and land on my tush, or die of embarrassment. What if they look at me?

My pale pink lipstick feels weird and sticky on my lips, and I hope my discount dress is presentable. Black and silky, the figure-skimming style gives the impression I'm sophisticated and experienced.

Ha. I wish.

I'm pure as driven snow after five years closeted in a boarding school so secure it could double as a jail. This is my first real job. My boss is tipped for the up-and-coming astrologist award, and I'll be there supporting her: organised, smiling, and utterly forgettable. Or I'll probably get the sack for being tardy and never convince anyone to trust the girl with no connections and no family.

I approach the stairs like they're a cliff. Wary, heart pounding, I stop.

It's not at all like a movie where the princess arrives at the head of the gold stairs and everyone is wowed. No. They're chatting and laughing, and not taking any notice of me, stuck at the top by my jittery nerves. I scan the crowd, delaying the inevitable, seeking Priscilla. It's a good vantage point here, I tell myself. That's why I've paused. If I can find her... My gaze locks with a man's.

It's a jolt. I grip the banister to stop myself from falling.

He's looking up at me from the far side of the ballroom, tall and impeccably dressed in a crisp dinner jacket. There are hundreds of people in that room, all ignoring me, but he gazes like we're the only two people in the world. Like he has been waiting for me, and only me.

Sebastian Laurent.

My heart stutters. It's been five years. His dark hair is shot with silver at the temples now, but he's otherwise the same. Broad shoulders, deceptively casual pose with his hands in his pockets. Maybe there are a couple of lines around his eyes. Laughter lines, or worry? I wish I knew.

But it's his regard that's most familiar. It's like he can see right through my skin and bone to read my soul.

Surely he doesn't recognise me?

He can't, it's impossible. Everything is different. I dye my hair a dirty blonde compared to my natural bright platinum, and I'm not a child anymore. And besides, we only met once.

What is Sebastian doing here? I descend the stairs, cheeks burning from his regard. His gaze is steady on my face.

I'm in shock. That's the only explanation for the blood zinging around my body and the lump in my throat. I never thought I'd see him again, and in real life he's so much more handsome than in the paparazzi photos. His eyes glitter in a way that can't be captured in an image.

But then I remember. He refused me as a child bride, but he still works with my family. I've seen pictures of him with my father at charity auctions and suchlike that evil men attend to sanitise their reputations. It's one thing to crush on the villain in a romance book; it's quite another to be faced with what a man will do for money.

He doesn't move as I reach the final step, but neither does he look away. It's like he's commanding me to come to him by sheer force of will. So I tilt my chin up and stare down Sebastian Laurent. He might be a powerful and dangerous mafia boss, but he doesn't own me, and I don't owe him.

I am a good girl now. I got out, and I'm not going back into that world. So I turn my head away. A dismissal.

I make my way through the well-dressed people discussing the position of Mars and the ascension of Venus. I understand snippets, but I'm still learning about astrology. I'm not sure if I believe all of it, but the idea that there's a predetermined future I just need to be in the right place to grab is appealing. And that people can be understood and put into neat categorisations. Virgo. Leo. Pisces. Your personality mapped out by your time of birth. I like the insight into people who I otherwise find confusing.

It takes me a while to find Priscilla and all the time I feel someone watching. Him.

The observation is a warm hand on the small of my back. Supportive. Comforting. Pushing me towards him. But he doesn't approach.

My boss is in the middle of a gaggle of women laughing about valentine's day and Scorpios, which I don't get but pretend to chuckle anyway. I creep in, trying to catch Priscilla's eye.

When she eventually notices, she gestures impatiently. "Where have you been?"

"Sorry—"

"Pay attention now you're finally here." She rattles off a list of appointments and I cram them into her online calendar via my phone. When I get to work tomorrow morning I will handwrite each item into her beautiful desk diary. Priscilla prefers the analogue versions of everything, even though it was my efforts on social media that gave her this big break. I still can't persuade her to do so much as one post herself. I do it all, and Priscilla, despite her initial scepticism, is gratifyingly dedicated to her online followers.

Once I'm caught up, I stand at the fringes of the group, listening and taking notes.

I say listening. I should be. But my mind won't focus. All my attention is on the little hairs on the back of my neck.

He's watching.

I turn occasionally, but I don't see him through the mass of elegantly garbed bodies.

If Sebastian knows who I am, he knows my worth. Not in money, he has plenty of that. He's a billionaire. But there is value to the ancient Carter family name, despite how long I've been gone.

I should be scared. A man I know to be a killer, a ruthless mafia kingpin who takes whatever he wants, is stalking me like I'm his prey.

He doesn't frighten me. The sensation of being watched warms me everywhere. It's the coat I didn't bring tonight, this feeling he's there. It's the blaze of a fire on chilled hands. I think if I slipped, or something happened, he'd notice. Would he be at my side in a second? Crazy as it sounds, I almost want to test him as we move into the dining room for the meal.

But then, why would he care about the girl he rejected for being too young, and everyone now thinks is dead? If he had demanded we wait until I was old enough to marry, would my father have accepted that, and not sold me off to Fletcher at sixteen? Back then, Laurent mafia needed the authority of Carter, and he could have achieved that with a long engagement. Instead, he murdered and gamed his way to power.

I guess we'll never know, but the possibility fuels a surge of righteous anger that obliterates any softer feelings. He's probably looking out of guilt. Shock. Horror at having to acknowledge the little lost princess.

Apparently my family claimed I was missing, presumed kidnapped and killed. Not good PR for it to get out that they practically sold me to Fletcher. And Laurent is their ally.

I might have looked at his picture in a magazine, but that doesn't mean I'm naive enough to think I want *him*.

It takes me a little time to check the seating plan and find Priscilla and my table. I guide her to it as everyone else has taken their seats. She's instructing me to post a photo of her I took with the Sagittarius constellation banner onto each of the social media sites and I'm nodding as we weave through the round tables, my bare elbow brushing on jackets draped over the backs of chairs and the swishy skirt of my dress catching on handbags. She really is peak Sagittarius.

I look up when I press submit on the photo to her account, and lurch to a halt.

Because at our table, grey eyes calm and observant, sits Sebastian Laurent.

2

SEBASTIAN

When our eyes meet, she jolts anew with recognition, her violet-blue eyes widening just as they did when she saw me from the top of the stairs. I manage a bland smile, but only because I've had time to compose myself.

Dressed in a demure but clingy black silk dress, her slender frame is too beautiful for words. Her hair is dyed that now-familiar toffee blonde and swept up in a neat chignon at the nape of her neck.

Juliet Carter was born to be my bride.

I must have her. I've always known, even when I lied to myself that I could keep away, that I would rearrange the heavens for us to be together. The connection is instant and undeniable.

Juliet Carter is *mine*.

But now she's Jeanette Capelle and can't be anything to do with me, however much I want her. She's out of this life and I will respect that.

"What are you doing here?" She slides into the chair next to me, gaze flicking between her name setting and my face.

"I have a great interest in astrology."

"No you don't."

"No, I don't." I can't help but smile. Some things haven't changed. She's still a mouthy brat and I adore it. "I'm here to wish you happy birthday." And protect her from whatever fuckwittery the Carter and Fletcher mafias have planned. "Twenty-one."

Jeanette has grown up into a siren with no vanity. She has the sort of beauty that compels a second glance. A casual observer might initially see her long hair and slim figure, but I see more. The titanium in her back. The determined tilt of her jaw. The uncertainty in her eyes.

"Tomorrow. You always did have bad timing." Her words are harsh, but she shifts her legs together under her dress and licks her lips. Her body is responding to mine without her awareness, turning towards me and when our gazes meet her pupils are blown.

Every cell in my body clamours for me to claim her.

"This event ends at midnight, so I'm only a few hours early," I say instead of taking her in my arms.

But when the clock strikes twelve the protective order I took out against her ex-husband and family runs out, and that is my only priority right now. Her safety.

We manage some polite conversation over dinner, and I can tell she wants to ask why I'm here, but can't bring herself to admit she doesn't already know. Part of her attention is on her boss, who barks orders to Jeanette even as she and every other person at the table tries to engage me in conversation about their nonsense. I'm used to it. Being rich trumps being lethal in most people's minds. They know I could have them quietly murdered but the lure of my patronage is greater inducement than fear of my power. I might just dispose of Jeanette's boss if she doesn't cease telling me about her social media following. That was what got us into this mess in the first place.

"Why do they need a fancy event to reveal their winners, if the results are pre-determined by constellations?" I ask Jeanette in an aside when there's the award for most improved something and Priscilla walks up to the podium and gushes about how much she loves all her followers.

"It's not like that." Jeanette rolls her eyes and answers from the side of her mouth. "It tells you about how you respond to events."

"So if you know my horoscope you know my personality? Based on when I was born?" I am, to say the least, sceptical.

"Yes. Ugh. I bet you're a Scorpio."

"Maybe."

"What star sign are you?" There's a hint of curiosity in the way she unconsciously leans into me.

"Haven't a clue." As head of the Laurent mafia, if I want to know the future, I *make* it. I don't read it in the stars.

Her pout, like she can't believe I'm not aware of this crucial piece of information, only succeeds in drawing my attention to her sweetly pink lips. "When's your birthday?"

"Twenty-ninth of March."

"Oh!" She looks me up and down. "That figures. Aries."

"What does that tell you about me?"

"Aries are born leaders. Impulsive. Domineering and energetic, you're highly assertive. Passionate, you know what you want and fear nothing in getting it."

"Huh." Maybe there is something in this whole zodiac thing. "What about you?"

There's a quiet point where someone is giving an acceptance speech and Jeanette leans over to whisper into my ear.

"Libras appreciate beauty, and are diplomatic. We're social, idealistic and lovers of justice."

Shivers go down my spine at her breath on my face. I turn slowly and our mouths are half an inch apart. Close enough to kiss.

"And are Aries and Libras compatible?"

Her mouth sets in a mulish line and I know. I just know... Under cover of applause, I say, "Very compatible, then."

"Yes," she admits.

The woman on the podium thanks everyone for coming and says the dance floor is open back in the ballroom. Several people head there as the music starts up and Jeanette casts them a longing glance.

"Come on." I stand and hold out my hand for her.

"What? I don't want to dance," she protests, but bites her lip and her eyes say the opposite.

"Yes, you do." And ridiculously, despite my never dancing, I'd like to with her.

She looks over to her boss who, seemingly placated by her award, gives Jeanette a gracious nod, and a word about having earned some fun. Jeanette's show of reluctance is belied by a barely hidden smile as she asks her boss to look after her purse, and gives me her hand.

Then her expression is back to wide-eyed shock as my fingers clasp over hers. The touch is hardly anything, but I feel it to my bones and obviously she does too.

Her hand is tiny in mine. Precious and small and I savour it as we walk into the group of dancers. Then, even better, I place a palm on her waist and pull her to me.

Not too close. Certainly not as close as I'd like, as I don't want to scare her.

It's an upbeat tune and I lead Jeanette into turns, lift her in spins, and dip her low over my arm. She tries to keep a straight face but only holds out for about thirty seconds because she clearly loves to dance. After that she's giggling and those violet eyes are sparkling like the faux stars on every wall and the ceiling.

The music merges into a slower dance and she steps into me with a shy smile.

Holding her in my arms is the missing words of a poem I've been repeating for my whole life. My very soul is at peace when I'm holding Juliet.

Jeanette.

Juliet was the child. Jeanette is this perfect young woman. Too young and beautiful for me, with my scarred body and ripped soul. She's untarnished by the world, despite all that happened to her. That sort of resilience takes my breath with admiration. She is stronger than anyone thought, including me.

It's only then I realise. She's an innocent.

There is no way she isn't a virgin. Not with the way she is learning to move with me, fitting herself to my sway with the music. She's discovering her body and how it feels when she's close to a man. I can see it in the inquisitiveness in her eyes and the softening of her stance.

I had feared Fletcher ruined her in some way before I got there, or maybe just scared her off the whole idea permanently, but no. She's still untouched and curious.

And that thought is an avalanche of relief for her and a fire of lust for myself. It's enticing in a way I didn't anticipate.

We keep dancing, in tune with each other and the

music. It's too easy. We go to the bar for water, twice, and Jeanette tells me about her extrovert but grumpy Sagittarius boss and predicts the star signs of my team based on what I tell her about them. Apparently my second-in-command is probably a Taurus. I'm entranced by her. I'm more delighted than can be contained in my chest that she talks to me like a friend. I crave hearing every thought that goes through this woman's mind.

And fool that I am, I don't interrupt her. I can't bring myself to spoil the mood of our enchanted evening until I absolutely have to. I want to be her prince charming until midnight. I ignore the two grunts in suits who appear at the bar, tracking Jeanette's every move. She doesn't notice them, as though she only has eyes for me.

We return to the dance floor when there's a pop song she likes and the back of my mind is cringing at the music. But Jeanette takes so much joy in it and we work so well together—a prelude to how we'll be in bed I'm sure—I don't care. I shove all thoughts aside.

During a slow song—the third in a row—she tilts her face to look into mine. I'm struck anew by her snub nose and the smattering of freckles on her cheekbones. And that's when I notice out of the corner of my eye a third of Fletcher's henchmen moving closer. Too close.

Ah damn. Reality was going to intrude sooner or later.

"Angel—" I cut her off mid-sentence about her little apartment. "You're in danger."

She tenses and I wish we were back at the fun—twirling so her skirt swooshes and she laughs helplessly—part of the evening.

"If I am, it's only because you're here."

I grit my teeth. I should have known this wouldn't be easy. "See that man in the corner?" I nod to the grunt in an ill-fitting black suit that hides a gun holstered around his chest.

She lifts her chin in a gesture I interpret as a yes.

"That's one of Ross Fletcher's men."

Fear goes through her eyes at the name of her ex-husband. I can see her trying to ascertain if I'm telling the truth. On the one hand, Fletcher drugged her and forced her into marriage. On the other, it has been five years since she saw anyone associated with her family's mafia. My arrival coincides with the appearance of Fletcher's men, and that's suspicious.

"Is he with you?"

"Things have changed." There used to be a trio of mafias that worked together. Then Laurent under my leadership became bigger, richer, more profitable. The tentative trust and peace broke down. "They want their lost princess back now they see a chance. Laurent is growing fast and it's causing tensions. Your father thinks having you found and reunited with Fletcher would cement their alliance." And Fletcher is still irate that his toy was taken away.

"They don't know where I am, or who," she protests. "I've been hiding for five years."

"Your cover is blown. They know your new name and where you are. There was a social media post you did about goats—"

"Capricorns."

"And you could be seen in the mirror." Just a small image of her, in one video, but with Jeanette sending all her boss' posts viral, she was recognised. A victim of her own talent and humble assumption no one would take any notice of her. Totally unaware of how gorgeous she is.

For a second I think she'll believe me. But then her innate modesty gets the better of her.

"They're not interested in me," she scoffs. "The lost princess."

"Not lost anymore."

She is still in my arms, but she's miles away. She doesn't believe me. Or rather, she doesn't want to believe me, but fears I might be right.

"Why should I trust you? You knew they were planning to marry me off. We got on well that one time we met, but you didn't *help* me."

The bitterness in her tone stings like salt on an open, festering wound. The injustice and truth of it knocks the air out of me.

I broke the arranged marriage between us after we met because she was sixteen. I'd never met her when I first agreed, assuming it would be a dull political arrangement. Then we met. I insisted on an afternoon to "get to know" my bride, and it revealed my mistake. She was a mouthy kid, as funny as she was unhappy, being coerced by her debt-laden father. I was having nothing to do with that shit. But I never anticipated they'd marry her off to Fletcher instead. He didn't have as much money as I did, but neither did he have as many morals.

As soon as I found out, I fought and burned bridges—physical and figurative—to rescue her.

But she's right. I should have known. No one else was protecting her, and we were friends during that afternoon. Weirdly united by shared disgust of the situation. I didn't see then what she would become, and how she needed me to wait for her. I was new to my kingpin job and too focused on my own affairs rather than keeping secure what was mine.

"You have to be careful. Lie low until I can deal with this. I have a safe house ready—"

"Another prison. You're not ordering me around," she bristles.

"Yeah, but I am." I failed to protect her before. I won't again.

We're not pretending to dance anymore. We're standing, her small hand in mine, inches apart, her staring up at me.

She shakes her head. "Sebastian Laurent," she murmurs. And then she does the last thing I expect. Boosting herself onto tiptoes, she kisses me right on the mouth.

It shocks the hell out of me. We were arguing? And now she wants to kiss me? It's a sweet kiss, no tongues or lingering intent. Just her lips pressed to mine. But before I can gather my wits and kiss her for real, she has drawn back.

"That was goodbye, Sebastian. I'm done with the mafia."

It's then that I notice two more Fletcher men at the edge of the dance floor. I check my watch.

Five past twelve.

Shit.

I got so caught up in being with Jeanette, I fucked up. I intended to get her out of here and safe before she turned twenty-one. Now our enemies are closing in and she hasn't agreed to let me protect her. "We're leaving."

"Sebastian!" She protests but my arm is firmly around her waist and she doesn't want to make a scene. I tow her through the ballroom and down the corridor leading to the back entrance where my armoured limo will be waiting to take her to a safe house.

"I'm not going." As we get into the empty corridor she digs her heels in.

I release her to get her to meet my eyes. "You don't understand the risks, Juliet—"

"Juliet is dead," she says coldly. "My name is Jeanette."

She turns away, towards the main lobby, and tosses over her shoulder, "Goodbye Mr Laurent."

Fletcher's man emerges from the ballroom and heads straight for Jeanette. I see what's about to happen with dreadful clarity; my angel is oblivious. I have a split second to make a decision as he reaches into his jacket for a weapon and I move faster.

Jeanette shrieks as my silenced bullet hits him just as he grabs for her. He crumples to the ground, groaning in pain.

In two steps I take first one of her wrists then her other and trap them in my one hand at the small of her back.

"What?!" She's in shock, staring at the slumped man, his gun loosely held and shoulder turning red.

"You're coming with me." No way am I letting this innocent girl be trapped back with her family and ex-husband. One arm around her ribcage, I bundle her out of the hotel side entrance, push her into the waiting limo and tug the door shut behind us.

"Let me go!" She tugs at her hands ineffectually and wobbles on her heels as the vehicle moves. Sitting, I pull her onto the seat next to me. The scent of her—roses—fills my head and makes me momentarily dizzy. As if I'm the captive, spun around blindfolded. But I keep my grip on her little wrists, so fragile in my big blunt fingers. It's then that she realises she has legs, and starts to kick me.

"Stop that or I'll tie you up." Fortunately—or unfortunately, whichever way you look at it—this limo is sometimes used for nefarious purposes.

"Make me," she hisses, and redoubles her efforts.

It's the work of a moment to shift so one of my hands

spans both of her wrists, and my leg is over her thighs. I refuse to acknowledge her slight body under mine, all tight skin and vibrating with anger as I flick open the compartment with bindings and secure Jeanette's hands together. She makes her ankles a little more difficult, and we both end up on the floor, me holding her calves down with my forearm while my logical mind tries to shut down in favour of the sensation of her skin on mine.

I ruthlessly suppress my inappropriate arousal and lean back, but at the sight of her it returns. Hands and feet bound, her eyes glitter with fury. And...

Surely not. I must be imagining it.

It can't be.

Her mouth opens in a pant but there's no fear in her eyes. She's... turned on.

3

JEANETTE

I glare at him.

He's... Ugh. I cannot.

I tug at my bonds, but they're tight. Sebastian Laurent doesn't do things by halves.

He huffs with irritation, as though it's *my* fault this has happened, and his gaze slides down my body, his expression serious and contemplative. I shiver with... I'd like to say cold. But it's not. It's the idea that he might like what he sees. Me, in a fancy dress, at his mercy.

My nipples pucker and though I try to ignore my body's reaction, I can't deny it. Being restrained by Sebastian Laurent is... Alright, it's hot af. I like it despite the panic and resentment and simple downright pissed-offness, I... Want him.

He lifts me onto the seat with surprisingly gentle hands after the force of tying me up, then settles opposite. Jaw working, eyes sparking with frustration, he stares in silence until his phone trills into life. He doesn't take his eyes off me as he answers with a snapped single word: his name. "Laurent."

Whatever he hears makes his brows lower into a scowl. "Send a team to deal with them. I want that safe house back."

Hanging up, he taps on the glass and speaks to the driver. All I catch is, "home".

There's a long silence, until eventually Sebastian says, "This isn't how I planned it."

"What do you want, a cookie?" I snip back at him.

"He'd have taken you to Fletcher at gunpoint."

That man. And the shiver this time is from fear. He had a gun, and he was coming right for me. I didn't see him until he'd almost grabbed me and if Sebastian hadn't been there...

The car comes to a stop and Sebastian doesn't hesitate. The door is open and he's lifting me, and I can't hang on or do anything but yell in annoyance as he tosses me over his shoulder.

"Put me down!"

He's carrying me like I'm a sack of spuds.

I thud my tied hands against his back and all that succeeds in is demonstrating to me he's all muscle. All warm, hard muscle that doesn't yield at all as I thwack him pointlessly with the sides of my wrists.

"No." His voice is more a rumble through my stomach than in my ears.

His arm is braced over the backs of my knees and... My butt must be about level with his face.

Oh god. No. No.

Book a decent guitar player for my funeral because I'm dying.

I've died. I'm dead.

The humiliation of Sebastian having his face right next to my butt as he carries me is the end.

Done.

Blood is rushing to my head and I have to hold myself up by pushing down on his buttocks to prevent myself from passing out. My breasts are hanging down and it must be the angle that makes my nipples feel tight. I barely notice the elevator, and when the doors slide open it isn't into a corridor like a normal person. No, it's into an elegant entrance hall as clearly he owns the whole floor. Sebastian doesn't stop until we're in a lounge with floor-to-ceiling windows looking out over the entirety of London.

He drops me onto a sofa and stands back, folding his arms. "Are you going to behave if I untie you?"

I shrug.

It's petulant, I know, but I have spent five years in an exclusive educational boarding prison—sorry, school—and I had just managed to get out into the real world. Now I'm at square one again.

"Sorry I had to restrain you," he says softly then pauses. Kneeling before me, he unties my ankles. I consider kicking him, but there's probably no point. All he'd do is tie me up again.

He frowns when I wince at him moving my foot. They're sore from dancing all night in those heels. With surprising dexterity, he removes my shoes, hissing as he sees the blisters.

"Those are going in the bin," he says in a voice like stone, tossing the shoes aside.

I don't object. Partly because I'm not in a position to argue here. But regardless, they hardly brought me luck, did they?

"I like your new name. Very French." His thumb slips against my bare leg in a caress so brief I wonder if I've imagined it.

"It was nothing to do with you." Not consciously. The

name I chose is a constant reminder of who I'm not. Of how alone I am. Not even a surname in common with anyone.

Then he unties my wrists and my skin tingles wherever his rougher, bigger hands touch mine. I take the opportunity to examine him. There are streaks of silver in his hair now that weren't there when I knew him before, but otherwise he's just as I remember. Gorgeous, dark, untouchable. Protective older man vibes.

"How old are you?"

He sits back onto his haunches, forearms on his knees. Steel eyes assess me. "Thirty-nine."

Too mature to be interested in a twenty-one-year-old lost princess. I'm imagining his interest, for sure. A figure of my overactive imagination.

I cannot believe that only yesterday I was furtively browsing the gossip columns and admiring the photos of Sebastian Laurent, wondering what my life would have been like if the stars had aligned differently. If we had met some other time, some other way. Would Sebastian be my husband now? That wasn't what I wanted five years ago, but tastes mature. Change.

Then *change back* when a man kidnaps you.

Mostly.

I rub my wrists where they're a little sore from the ropes. But despite the pain, I know if I was with Fletcher things would be much worse. "Why did you help me?"

"Curious now, are you?"

"Kidnappy now, are you? One of these things is illegal." Because saving me from Fletcher and being handsome doesn't make him the good guy.

He sighs. "Okay. I'll answer."

"Truthfully?" I'm suspicious.

"Yes. If you stay here."

"Just stay. Like a dog or a china doll... Sit around." I give a growl of exasperation and stand abruptly. I stride to the window and look out over London, the glow of life and excitement. Barred to me, as usual. "That is all I was destined for as the Carter princess, all I've been allowed to do for five years, and all you want me to do now."

The windows disappear below the surface, giving the impression you could step straight out into the air and walk until you notice the lack of floor, like a Looney Tunes character. Vertigo tugs at me as I look down.

I step right to the edge, toes millimetres from the glass. My breath fogs the black and twinkling yellow lights of the city.

It's a silly urge, but I place my palms on the window and push. In a movie I'd be able to throw myself through the glass or open it and fly away. But this is real life, so it's perfectly immovable. My next gilded cage.

Sebastian appears next to me. In the reflection I see his bow tie is now loose around his neck and his top button is undone, revealing that dip between the collarbones.

It's... Compelling. I wonder how it would feel to touch my thumb into the curve.

I look back at the city.

"It's beautiful. The night skyline," I say. Those lights represent millions of people, far away. Not even one who really *cares* about me. At least if I was at home in my tiny flat I could chat with my new astrology friends on social media and not feel so isolated.

"Beautiful, yes." But Sebastian's voice is a caress, not at all like he's admiring the night sky. "I understand why you want independence—"

"No!" I turn on him. "You don't. You've always been able to do whatever you wanted. You were the heir then the head of Laurent. You had the freedom to choose. I—I had nothing to do but wait to be sold off as a bride. When I fought against that, my father just sold me quicker. Years of protective custody and education. And finally—finally—I have a job I'm good at after graduating. I'll lose it if I don't turn up for work. So, no." My chest is heaving as I pour out my frustration. Tears threaten at the corner of my eyes. "You *don't* understand. I nearly got taken by that man. I couldn't stop you from kidnapping me. I couldn't stop Fletcher when he came for me years ago. I thought I was safe, and I don't want to be a helpless princess any longer." *Lost.*

He's silent.

"I'll make you a deal," he says eventually. His grey eyes are soft now. "I'll teach you to defend yourself from me, or someone like me, trying to do anything you don't want to do. And I'll answer your questions. All of them. And in return, I want you to remain here for one day. Until Midnight tomorrow."

One day. "But my job."

"I'll call in sick for you. Your boss will understand for a single day."

"A day alone in your apartment." What a dreary prospect. More of just me and four walls. I can never sleep on my own in a new place, so bonus I'll be miserable *and* knackered.

"Not alone." My heart jumps. "I'll phone in sick too."

"To who? You're a mafia kingpin."

"A higher authority. You perhaps." He winks.

I can't help but smile wryly. Sebastian is putting business on hold to kidnap me.

Me. The lost princess everyone had forgotten about.

Except maybe Sebastian didn't? He's looking at me like he's trying to tattoo my image onto his retinas.

Though perhaps I'm imagining that. I'm not good at attracting sincere affection or interest. Exhibit A: my father who only used me in his power games. Exhibit B: my ex-husband. Exhibit C: my innocence.

Sebastian is the first man to touch me and that was because he was *kidnapping* me.

"Alright."

Sebastian smiles wide and genuine, his eyes twinkling. As though twenty-four hours with me is a treat rather than a bind. I stare at him and remember the second when I thought Fletcher's man would take me. The sheer bolt of terror and the quiver of helplessness. Maybe I'm naive, but I think Sebastian is genuinely trying to protect me.

"What would you like to learn first?" he asks softly.

Teach me how to kiss, I almost say. *Teach me how to make you come apart at the seams. Show me how to make my body sing.*

"You snatched me from behind. I want to know how to stop that happening."

I'll not be a victim again. Not of Sebastian, or anyone else.

4

JEANETTE

He nods, all seriousness again. "Face the window."

This is a self-defence class; there shouldn't be anything sexy about it. But despite myself my skin thrums with the knowledge he will touch me. He makes my body warm and liquid and weak. How I'm going to pretend I'm fighting him off, when I want to draw him close, I don't know.

"I'll be able to see you in the reflection," I protest but do as he says.

"Close your eyes."

Oh. Yeah, obvious solution.

But with my eyes closed, every other sense is heightened. I hear the slight soft sounds of his clothes as he moves. I can smell his scent, stronger now I'm allowing myself to acknowledge it. He smells like sea rocks and green oranges. He smells like one of those massive photographs of a blue-green wave feels.

"I'm going to touch you."

I jump a little because his voice is much closer than I thought, and his breath is warm on the curve of my ear.

"Where?" I squeak.

"I'll grab your wrist."

My wrists are suddenly the centre of my universe. I have no blood anywhere else in my body. Certainly not in my head, where it belongs, to help me make rational decisions. Because if it was, I would be screaming that this was a bad idea. That some unattractive man who doesn't set me on fire with need should teach me to get away, not Sebastian.

"Just respond as you would naturally," he says and the next moment his fingers grip my wrist. I gasp and freeze. That's my instinctive response. Then panic sets in, prickly and jagged under my skin. I twist towards the window, but obviously that's a window and I smack right into the glass with an undignified grunt.

He releases me instantly. "Good."

"Not good," I huff, my heart hammering in my chest as I turn to him.

"It was." He nods encouragingly and am I imagining something dark in his gaze? "You didn't just accept it." Which is what I did earlier, he's too tactful to point out. "You need to fight back. Go for sensitive areas. Eyes. Nose." I look at the corresponding places on his body. "Groin."

My gaze slips down without my volition and oh no now I am blushing furiously.

I cannot. I cannot look at Sebastian, look away from the line of his cock beneath that expensive fabric, or do anything other than be a completely inexperienced girl who is fascinated by a real man.

It looks big. Huge. His trousers are slightly tented and OMG does he... Surely not from touching *me*? But I really don't know what it would be like, or how—um—engorged—please tell me I didn't just think that word—it would get.

Maybe his underwear is like... Thermal or something? Because there's no way—

"Next time try going the other way." His gravelly voice sends tingles through me and I manage to drag my gaze from his nether regions, but I can't meet his eyes. "Dig your elbow into me and bounce off rather than pulling away, which is what I expect."

"Yep," I squeak.

He knows I was looking at his cock. Or desperately trying to, like if I could have X-ray vision to look under his clothes I would totally be gawping at my first naked man right now.

"Again?" he says mildly.

We resume our positions. My pulse is so loud it's like a nightclub downstairs as I wait for him to grab me. The anticipation is... exciting. Knowing it's Sebastian means this is the best sort of thrilling. It's walking a tightrope with a safety net. The exact amount of danger to make me feel more alive than I ever have before, but also I know he won't hurt me.

I guess I have no justification for that belief, but I have it all the same. It's bone-deep. This man refused to hurt me when I was sixteen, and instead found influence the hard way. He danced with me, and shot a man I'm certain meant me harm. Something tells me Sebastian wouldn't take advantage.

Even if perhaps I wouldn't mind if he did. Now. Just a little.

I yelp when he pins my hand to my side this time. I try to headbutt him. It's pointless, as he's a head taller than I am and all that happens is my skull connects with his chest as I turn into him. For half a second all of my front is pressed to his, while he holds my wrist behind my back.

My body responds like a match struck. Shivers go down my spine and spread heat between my legs even as I move all the way around and wrench from his grasp.

I'm wheezing from the exertion and adrenaline as I face him. I can feel the flush in my cheeks.

And he's... Not affected. Or is he? His grey eyes are dark and intense like a long summer evening shadow.

"Okay," I say after a moment. I swallow hard and step towards him. "I think I have that now."

Total lie. I have no idea what I'm doing, and I'm about to take this into territory I have even less experience in. "And what do I do if my attacker is from the front?"

He's so much taller than me, this close I'll get a crick in my neck looking at him. But I don't care. I feel... Reckless. Weirdly safe. It's as though there are no consequences here. There's no tomorrow, or mafia politics, or anyone else. It's just him and me and all the things he could teach me.

Not just self-defence.

"As I said before." Husky, so husky, like he's forcing out the words through a dozen combs. His gaze doesn't leave mine. "Go for sensitive areas."

"Here." I skim my palm onto his groin area and my eyes go wide as I feel how hard and hot he is. That is *definitely* an erection. And I did it to him. This game we've been playing has made him hard. "Plus eyes and nose, didn't you say?" My voice is a sigh. Hardly there at all. I reach my other hand up, meaning to touch his cheek and drift over his eyes. Not to hurt him, but... maybe just to see how he feels beneath my fingertips. Find out what he does. But my fingers catch at the join between his neck and jaw and I'm entranced. I can't move on.

That line between the soft skin and abrasive stubble. That black beard growth is so masculine, and the hot rigid length of his cock under his trousers is the balance to him here. Both unyielding and also smooth. He's like nothing I've ever known. Every part of him is different to my body and yet I know we'd fit.

My hand spans maybe a third of his neck. I can feel his pulse, vital and strong beneath my fingers. I have no idea why it's so good to feel him like this. There's a power in him allowing me to. Because the only reason I'm touching Sebastian is because he is permitting it. He's passing over the control to me.

"Are you the attacker now?" The corner of his mouth quirks up. "Going to choke me to death?"

"Maybe." I tighten my grip. "To make you release me."

"You don't need to strangle me for that. Just wait until the danger has passed. When it's safe, I'll let you go."

"I thought you said tomorrow." I'm stroking his neck and his pause says we both know it. I'm *caressing* him shamelessly, pushing his shirt collar away to access his shoulder and sweeping up to his jaw. He's the most beautiful man I've seen. I want to explore every part of him.

"You're the only one who could," he whispers. "I'd let you and only ask that you stay safe and happy."

That stills me.

"Really?"

"Seeing you as bright as the sun. Incandescent. It's all I ever wanted for you."

"You'd let me..." My brain is overwhelmed by the thought, stuck spinning like a computer trying to do too many things. "What would you do if you were caught and someone else had their fingers around your throat?" I bring my other hand up to demonstrate.

"I'd regain the advantage," he whispers.

"How? When they were choking you?" I squeeze the

smallest amount with both hands. I'm teasing a deadly predator.

"Like this."

He bats my arms away from the elbow outwards, forcing me to release him. Then he grabs my hips and the next thing I know I'm pinned to the cool glass, my back to his front.

The air has been knocked from my lungs, but not in a nefarious way. In an, *oh-god, that is his cock pushing into my lower back and he's hard as a steel rod*, way. And the tips of his fingers are pressing onto the little mound of my pubic bone. Close, so close to where I need him. His hand slips down and cups my pussy through the silk of my dress and my knickers underneath.

"I can feel your heat, angel." His whisper ripples through me.

There are witty retorts or clever moves or sultry phrases that I'll think of later, but right now I'm incapable. I tilt my hips to attempt to get a fraction more of his fingers on me.

"You know how to fight me off from here." A stark instruction.

"Yes." I could make him stop. I could kick his shins or go for his eyes. If I reached for his cock I bet he'd step away. I suspect if I just said no—or the first letter, *nuh*—he'd release me immediately.

One word with two letters. Any other girl, not wanton or slutty like me, would use that word.

I don't do any of those things.

I let out a little whimper.

Because I don't want him to stop.

5

SEBASTIAN

I give her a few seconds to knee me in my already blue balls. Several more to be certain. Then every possessive instinct in me is unleashed.

She's mine to please, for now.

"Lift your skirt."

She hesitates. "But the window... Anybody could see..."

"Uh huh. Have you got knickers on, or is your sweet little pussy going to be exposed to all of London?"

We're far too high up for anyone to see, but the hitch in her breathing suggests that's not a barrier to her enjoying the game.

There's a rustle of fabric as she drags up the silk. It rucks around my hand and I glide my palm to the naked skin of her thighs, exploring until I touch cotton. I almost laugh. Of course my girl has cotton knickers on. I bet they're white too.

"So sweet..." I push the waistband of her knickers aside and slide my fingers in. She's so wet it's seeping out of her slit, soaking before I've even touched her. I can't hold back a groan. "And yet so needy. Spread your legs, angel. Bare yourself to me."

I nudge her inner thigh with my knee and she shifts her legs further apart. And that's what I want. Her willing compliance after her spirited fight.

I reach further into that silk. Her folds are plump, swollen with need. I push through until I find her pearl and stroke it.

She makes a little keening sound and my cock, if possible, gets even harder. I circle her clit with two fingers and she leans back into me. The scent of her is part roses and part pure arousal. She fills my senses, too delicious.

"No one else has done this, have they? Touched you here," I demand.

She shakes her head.

A lion in my chest roars, *yes*.

I want to be her first everything. I don't know how I'm going to let her go tomorrow, or how I'll survive the rest of my life without her. This day I've bargained for will have to feed years of desire. A memory to sustain me like dwindling rations eked out by an apocalypse survivor.

My other hand creeps around to the slinky front of her dress, pushing it off her shoulders and to the swell of her breasts. She's not wearing a bra, and hell but I like that. Small but perfectly formed, her tits are perfect. I cup one and brush my thumb over her nipple. It perks under my ministrations, and I love how responsive she is, like her body is attuned to mine.

She's tucked into me now, her back pressed to my chest and trapped on the other side by the glass.

I make rhythmic circles over her clit, listening to her soft moans as I give her exactly the escalation of pressure she needs, pinching her nipple too.

That squirm of her bottom into the top of my thighs is tantalising. Much as my cock insists on attention, and it's tempting to rub myself into the small of her back, I don't. Her pleasure is all that matters. I could wrap my hand around my cock on my own later and think of her—though I won't do that either—but I only have this one opportunity to give her this. For the first time, too. There will only be once that she has never before come with a man. I want it to be with me, and it has to be spectacular.

I'm succeeding. She's disintegrating in my arms, shaking with the intensity, slumped back against me, her honey waterfall of hair over my chest. But she's not there yet, and though rubbing her this way is a simple but effective way to bring her to orgasm, I can do more. One advantage of big hands.

I shift my fingers down so the heel of my thumb covers all of her clit and I slip my forefinger deep into her heated wet folds, and then... There. I push into her tight passage as I press onto her clit.

That does it. She breaks, clenching around my finger and writhing as pulse after pulse of her orgasm overtakes her. Her soft moans fill up my soul as I ease her through it, thrusting my finger in and out. I hold her and whisper that she's doing well and I'm proud of her, like she's bearing a trial. But she comes so intensely, I suspect it might feel like an ordeal. It's minutes until she begins to hold her own weight again.

I let her inch away, even as every one of my limbs clamours that she remain with me, and that we do that repeatedly. At very least, I wish she'd turn and kiss me.

She doesn't. Her cheeks flush and she drops her skirt. I remove my hand from her knickers, but smooth my palm over her mound as I release her. A promise. I'll be back for more, as soon as I can.

"Sorry," she mutters, and looks away.

"No." I grab her chin and make her look at me. "None of that." My voice is stony, even to my own ears. "You don't apologise to me for what I did."

"But I didn't... You're—"

"I don't know who told you that you had to say sorry, or be ashamed for wanting something for yourself." Though I could guess. Her father. "You accepted what was offered. You don't have to give back to deserve what should be yours by rights. Not with me. Never again, you hear?"

As she nods there's a fight of emotions on her face. Relief, embarrassment, disbelief and happiness are the ones I see, but she's a kaleidoscope. Everything, this girl. But there is one emotion I don't see, and that makes my heart glad.

She's not afraid.

"Should we resume our lesson?" she asks.

It's so late it'll be dawn in only a few hours. We only have one day together, and though I want to savour it, I should let her rest.

"That's enough for one night." I step back from her before I decide to do something truly misguided, like lie her onto the sofa and push into that soft pink slit, fucking her until she moans my name and comes on my cock. "Take the first room on the right in the hall." It's the mirror room of mine.

She hesitates and smooths her hand down her silk-covered thigh. "I don't have anything to wear to bed."

Sweet girl. It doesn't even occur to her that she could sleep naked, as she would if she were with me. Or even that she could just keep on those cute little knickers.

I catch her small hand in mine and walk to my bedroom. Though it's tempting to invite her in, I leave her in the hallway, grab a shirt from the wardrobe and bring it to her.

"G'night." She clutches the shirt to her chest and smiles wistfully.

"Sleep well, angel."

Then there's a door between us and I have never wished as fervently as I do now that I lived in a tiny cabin with only one bed.

But that's not happening.

Neither is sleep, for me. I grab a bottle of Scotch and pour myself a generous measure. The likelihood of my sinking into dreams is about five per cent higher after a nightcap, so I figure it's worth a try. Maybe it'll get the sunshine and roses smell of Jeanette's hair out of my nose.

I sit with my laptop, sip my drink and wonder what I did in a past life to deserve this torture of having Jeanette in my home, without being able to claim her.

It's all the fault of my overactive conscience. A bloody bind for a mafia kingpin. Any other man would take what she doesn't even realise she is offering.

I check up on my investments, who of my people have paid, and what the status of my territory's peace is. But apart from some goons at the safe house, it's quiet. Too quiet.

Fletcher and Carter know I took Jeanette, and I'm expecting there to be fallout. But so far, no one is acknowledging she's anything other than a pretty twenty-one-year-old.

Suits me.

Linda—my second-in-command—drops off some clothes for Jeanette. I don't examine too carefully why I brush off her assertion that Jeanette should have some female company her own age. Instead I snap that if she wants to argue with me, she can return to working for Fletcher.

Obviously she shuts up then. And I feel bad, because whatever happened I wouldn't send her back to them after the way Fletcher treated her. But not bad enough to allow her to intrude on my time with Jeanette.

The lights are so low it's almost completely dark and I'm into my second whisky—one was never going to get me close to sleep with my mind constantly gravitating to Jeanette—when there are soft footsteps in the hallway to the bedrooms.

Jeanette.

Will she try to escape? I'm curious about whether she'll head for the elevator despite our bargain, and what she'll do when she finds it pin locked. I almost want her to attempt it, for the excuse to touch her again when I catch her. The air is steam, burning my throat as I wait to see what she'll do.

She pushes the door into the main living space open, and the air cools.

I'd prefer if she didn't notice me so I would get to enjoy the sight of her long legs and possessive glee that she's wearing nothing but my shirt. Her hair is in a loose plait over her shoulder and she looks sweet enough to make my teeth ache.

But instead her gaze finds me like she can sense my presence.

"Oh! Sorry!" She shrinks back.

"It's alright."

"I didn't mean to disturb you. I couldn't sleep, and I thought..." she trails off. "Couldn't you sleep either?"

"Why can't you sleep, angel?" I don't answer her question, partly because it's obvious. Partly because I can't explain to this innocent girl that the reason I can't sleep is her.

"I can never sleep in a new place on my own."

That's an arrow to my heart. How many new places has she been, alone, since I saw her five years ago? Too many. How many nights has she been unable to sleep? One would be more than I would accept.

I imagined getting her out was enough. It never occurred to me that the posh boarding school would leave her as lonely as I've been all these years. Guilt sticks in my throat.

"I thought I'd get something to drink," she adds.

"Of course." I'm up in a second. This is easy to fix. "I have hot chocolate."

That's the right thing to suggest, as she gives me a shy smile of thanks.

She looks slight and vulnerable in the oversized shirt, and a little rumpled from tossing and turning in bed. She fiddles with the turned cuffs—still too long—as we stand in the kitchen, waiting for the kettle.

I should tell her about the clothes I've acquired for her, but I kid myself that it's the middle of the night and it would be better to do that in the morning. In actual fact, the reason is I love seeing her in my shirt too much to suggest she change.

"Are you going to bed now?" she asks when the mug is in her hands. She takes a cautious sip and those massive violet eyes pin me.

I promised her the truth, but I nod. I *should* go to bed. Any more of her this evening will cement her in my heart so firmly I'll be chiselling her out until the end of time after she leaves tomorrow. But if we stay up all night together I'll be tempted to take her, and so I can't let her think it's an option to sit with me.

She grips the mug harder.

"Can I sleep in your room?" she asks with a rush.

My chest tightens like I've been punched.

"Why?"

Her white upper teeth capture her pink lower lip and she looks at her hot chocolate as though the answer is there. "I sleep better with someone else."

My expression must darken to thunder as she hastens to add, "Not like that. Just I always shared a room at school. I have my own place now, but only for a few months and I'm not used to it yet. I usually leave the television on so I don't feel... But there isn't one in that bedroom here. And I'm... I... I don't want to be alone tonight. The first of my adult life."

Will this ache in my chest ever cease? I suspect not.

"I only have one bed."

"Then can I..." She looks at me from under those excessively long dark lashes. "Sleep in your bed?"

This is going to kill me. But I will never deny Jeanette anything.

"Yes."

Her face brightens.

It's not like I'll sleep anyway. One of us might as well.

"Where's your bedroom?"

Wordlessly, I lead her there.

"Oh! It's gorgeous!"

It's painted a deep violet blue, the colour of her eyes, and lined with bookshelves. I suppose it is beautiful, if you like books and blue.

"Get in, I'll join you," I direct.

She obeys and well, there goes my cock again, pulsing as

she pulls back the covers and slips under the duvet of my bed. I am the worst. Lusting after a girl half my age. Yes, one who came on my fingers earlier, but seriously? I need to get a grip. And not a grip around my cock, which is what I'm tempted to go to the shower and do. Take the edge off.

Instead I strip down to my boxers, throw on a T-shirt so there's another layer of buffer between us, and flick out the light. But not before I've seen her watching me, taking in my momentarily bare chest with wide eyes.

She shifts as soon as I've laid down, and yep, she snuggles into me. I'm a scary mafia kingpin and she's unafraid. I cautiously wrap my arms around her, and she sighs with contentment and I swear within a minute her breathing has evened out and she's asleep.

Brat.

She's left me with a hard-on and a heart so full of her it might burst at any moment.

And tomorrow? My heart will definitely explode into tiny broken shards. Because much as she's comfortable, soft and sleepy in my arms now, she wants her freedom. For that, she needs to be far from London. And from me.

I have to let her go.

6

JEANETTE

I wake up alone in an unfamiliar blue room full of books, with the feeling something momentous has changed. Possibly, me. I think Sebastian changed me at a cellular level when he made me come yesterday. My body feels like there's liquid glitter swooshing through, pumped by my heart.

I didn't know it could be like that.

Really, legitimately, I should be afraid. Instead I feel like I'm in Beauty and the Beast. This is a bedroom made for me, and this whole place is enchanted. When I find an open suitcase full of clothes in my size, the feeling only heightens.

Swiftly followed with irritation.

There's no magic here. Just Sebastian Laurent.

The bastard planned this? He happens to have clothing exactly to my tastes, that fit perfectly?

All these clothes are perfect colours, flattering styles. More luxurious than I could afford for myself, but how did he know from one blurry photo that I like blue dresses? He needs to explain what's going on, stat. Yes, I liked the orgasm, yes, I slept well in his arms. But none of that means anything when it seems he schemed to capture me.

I drag on the first clothes I find in the case: white underwear, a pair of jeans, and a pretty cotton top.

It takes me finding four bedrooms, an office, a movie room, a snug, two lounges, and a library until I eventually discover Sebastian in a gym with a swimming pool. He's on the treadmill, sweat gleaming on his tanned skin, earbuds in, and top off.

I stare. And stare.

His body is... And it makes mine...

I know that some men look fit, in an abstract way. I've seen films, and peeked at the internet once or twice. But I had no idea seeing a man in real life would be like an earthquake in my nether regions. I saw him last night, but not like this. A brief snapshot of his chest before it was covered is not the same thing as his back on display, all rippling muscles and shoulders I want to cling to as he... My imagination can't supply the details, and my experience definitely is insufficient.

What would it be like to touch his back? Yes, he's sweaty, but—and I know this sounds deranged—I want to lick him. I've gone gooey inside just from looking at him, what if he took that powerful body and held it above me, trapped me under him...

"Jeanette?"

My chin snaps up. He's looking over his shoulder at me, amusement curling his lips. Slowing the treadmill, he grabs a towel to mop up—I have to swallow the urge to ask if he needs help with that—and then tugs a T-shirt on before coming to stand before me.

"You okay?"

I'm certain there was a reason I came to find him. I'm pretty sure before I melted, I was pissed off at him.

Like *really* annoyed.

"Glad the clothes fit," he comments when more seconds pass and my brain is still stuck on how physically beautiful he is.

Yes! That was it! The pique flows back.

"You had clothes ready. You planned this. What the fuck, Sebastian? Why did you plan to kidnap me?"

"I didn't intend to kidnap you." And he's such a damn good liar, he sounds sincere.

"Truth, Mr Laurent. Or do your bargains mean nothing to you? In which case..." I turn to find an exit. Or at least a window I can... not be able to throw myself out of.

"No." He grabs my wrist and this time I instinctively twist and stomp down on his foot as I aim the heel of my hand at his nose. He catches my arm millimetres from impact and I grunt with rage as I try to knee him in the balls, but he dodges.

"Better." He smiles and it's all the way up to his eyes. "You would have hurt anyone else."

"I wanted to hurt *you*. Because despite what you said, *you* are the one who has kidnapped me."

He's still holding my arms and again, I shouldn't like the feel of him, but apparently my limbs have not moved on from seeing him half naked and sweaty.

"Are you always this grumpy before you've had coffee?" He releases me and steps away before I can do anything violent with those free weights in the corner. Though, I doubt I'd be able to even lift most of them.

"Come on. Coffee and presents first, then explanations."

I follow him into the kitchen and grit my teeth as he takes forever to make, admittedly delicious-smelling coffee.

"That's for you," he says as he leans against the counter and I peer over the coffee mug at him from my place on the other side. Adversaries.

I pick up the neatly wrapped book shaped object and finger the paper. It's been a long time since anyone gave me a birthday present. I glance up at him suspiciously, but he smiles and sips his coffee.

I slip my finger under the paper's edge and carefully unwrap a pretty hardbound notebook. The pages inside are luxurious and thick. My throat clogs. It's pretty.

"Thank you."

"That's not strictly your present. Open it to the front inner cover."

I do as he says, and find a set of numbers and an address. Huh?

"That's a bank account I've opened in your name. It has some money in it. Anytime that money dips below that amount, I'll top it up."

"What? Like an infinite refill? Like I could withdraw all the money every day and eventually be able to like, buy a house or something?"

He chuckles. "It wouldn't take a year. Nothing like that long."

"You're giving me money?"

"I'm giving you a safety net," he states softly.

"This is your way of keeping track of me." That realisation is... Weirdly comforting? I should be scared, but I'm not.

He shrugs. "If you don't use it, I won't be able to track you. There's no tracking on the book. But if you use the account, yeah. I'll know."

I put down the notebook and nod grimly. Do I like this? Maybe. It's a kind gesture, if a bit over the top. There is part of this that bothers me though. "So you did plan all this. Like I said."

"You weren't supposed to come here."

"You have another location for your kidnappees." I'm not jealous. I'm not.

"Will you let me finish, angel?" A touch of exasperation threads his words.

I drink my coffee sulkily.

"You won't be safe until Fletcher is dead, and even then, I think your father would claim you back. All those years away, with a new name, were supposed to protect you. Make you unrecognisable."

I shrug. "I am."

"You might have been if you were on the street. But then your boss got famous..." He makes a fait accompli gesture.

"I did that," I admit.

"Impressive." He nods. "And foolish."

"I didn't know it would get me into the limelight! And so what if it did? It's been a long time."

"Hey," he says soothingly. "I said I'm impressed. But that reflection of you in the mirror? Something like it was going to happen. Eventually."

I may be a little touchy about this. Being told most of your life that you're a silly girl will do that. "I guess."

"I had a safe house prepared for you. I intended to give you a place to go, before you were twenty-one. But..." He folds his arms. "I got a bit carried away, enjoying your company, and didn't explain until it was too close to midnight to do anything less than swiftly. And you weren't as cooperative as I'd hoped."

"I might have been more understanding if you'd explained better," I snap.

"Yes."

And I have to give him credit, he accepts his portion of the blame with grace. Though the reality is, we were both distracted by how well we were getting on and the attraction that clicked into place.

"Then the safe house had been compromised. I couldn't send you there. I didn't plan to kidnap you, just give you somewhere secure until I could fix the threat."

"You've had five years!"

"No, I've had one day."

The photo showing me in the mirror. It was yesterday.

Darn it. He's right.

"Before that my plan was to let you live your life and just keep an eye out for any trouble. I knew your father and Fletcher wanted to get you, but they had no idea where you were before that goat video."

"Capricorn," I mutter.

"Yes, that one. I did try to murder your whole family and Fletcher before your birthday, but the idea turned out to have some logistical problems that would take a little longer," he says neutrally, as though he was discussing ordering pizza for dinner. "Hence..."

"The kidnap."

"The plan to get you away from danger," he corrects gently.

A normal person would be at least slightly horrified by the concept of a man murdering people to protect her... Apparently I'm not as normal as I thought. Because although I'd rather people didn't die, the plain way Sebastian says that he'd do terrible things to defend me makes my skin warm. He's massive and deadly and scary and he is ruthlessly using his power to care for me.

"Felt a lot like abduction," I grumble. I probably need more coffee.

"I'll bear that feedback in mind for another time." Amusement lights his eyes into silver.

I scowl. "You're making a habit of stealing women." I do not like the thought of him taking anyone else. I am... Envious of his hypothetical victims.

Now he's outright smiling. "Only you. And I'll treat you very well."

"Feed me?" Because I haven't eaten since dinner last night and after everything that's happened, I'm ravenous.

"I'll make you breakfast, angel." He turns his attention to pulling ingredients from the fridge and a couple of minutes later places a cup of tea at my elbow.

"What are you cooking?" That isn't the question I want an answer to, but I'm too scared of rejection to ask why he was content to give me an orgasm last night then continue as though nothing has happened.

"My speciality, full English breakfast."

"That's your speciality?" It seems too simple for him somehow, but the warmth of the steaming mug of tea in my hands is comforting. A paradox, like him.

"Uh huh. I'll tell you a secret."

"You'll tell me all your secrets, you promised." Including why he didn't take the opportunity to have sex with me last night in bed, or for me to return the favour at least.

"Yep. But you wouldn't know to ask for this one. Breakfast is the only meal I know how to cook. That's why it's my speciality."

I watch him work in silence. He says he can't cook, but

he's as in control in the kitchen as he is anywhere else. Like his hands have dexterity and knowledge whether he's playing my body like an instrument, killing a man who threatened me in cold blood, or slicing tomatoes with a gleaming blade. He gives a sharp "no" when I ask if I can help.

The smell is divine. By the time he places food before me, my mouth is watering from the oily tang of bacon and stuffy-sweet carbohydrates.

"That is enormous. It's enough food for a week." Fried eggs, sausage, bacon, mushrooms, tomatoes, baked beans and a hash brown cover the plate. There's toast on the side and he replaces my mug of tea with a new one.

"Need to keep your energy up."

"So I can escape?" I bite into a piece of hot butter-covered toast and almost moan at how good it is.

"For our lessons." There's a flickering emotion in his eyes so brief I can't read it. "We have the whole day for me to teach you to defend yourself."

His plate has twice as much food as mine, but he eats it with steady, measured focus.

"And answer all my questions." I think about *that* question. Why doesn't he want to touch me again? I'm his prisoner. He could do whatever he wanted.

"I'll always answer for you, angel."

I'm not brave enough to ask, so I slide into the easier—easier?!—topic of why I'm his captive.

"If you're here, do I take that to mean you're not currently disposing of… the leaders of Carter and Fletcher." I can't quite bring myself to say, my father and ex-husband.

"Plans are being put in place." He's finished his food and sits back to watch me.

"Oh." So I'm not stuck here forever. That's... Good, right?

"Why? Do you want me to spare their lives?"

I think of how little I meant to any of them. But I surely should be better...

"They don't deserve your compassion, angel. You're not the only girl they have hurt."

"But..."

"If you'd prefer them to live, I'll see what can be arranged." He says it like it would be a concession. Like unless I intervene they're as good as chopped meat.

"I can decide?" Another gift. Or another favour? It's a little thrill to have the power of life or death over those who once held it over me, and chose to sell me off. I don't know what to do with the sensation. It's wrong, and yet... Like everything with Sebastian, it's right. He hands over the control to me, even though I'm his prisoner.

He tilts his head. "Yes. But I'll want something from you in return."

7

SEBASTIAN

"What do you want?" There's a hint of anticipation as well as question in her eyes, but no wariness now.

It's tempting to admit, *her*.

I could reveal the depth of my adoration with one word. And perhaps she'd give me her body for the day, or the night. I think that curiosity in her expression might get the better of her, and she'd allow me to steal away her innocence. I'd love to. My cock demands I take her with every throb of blood through it. Yes, I want to give her release, and it soothes my soul to do that. Joining us would be even sweeter. Stroking into her for my pleasure as well as hers, having her tighten around me and come on my cock.

But I won't bargain for her love. I only want that freely given and forever.

Neither will I allow my baser urges to wreck me, or harm her. If I have her, she'll be *mine*. But she deserves the choice of liberty. I won't coerce her into being with me, however much I might want it. I am enough of a bastard to take her virginity; I'm not so immoral as to steal her for my own without her knowing.

I can't help the bone-deep feeling that she's mine, but I can let her decide, keep her out of harm's way, for now at least.

"Don't leave until either they're dead, or I've found a new safe house for you," I say.

"You want me to stay?"

Always. Forever. I want her by my side and in my bed. "Just until you're safe."

She'd be safer with me.

Those trusting blue eyes peek out from under her long lashes. When did she start to have such faith in me? She puts down her knife and fork, and traces a pattern on the worktop with her fingertip, thinking, white teeth pressing onto that plush pink bottom lip.

"But you won't be able to keep me safe until I've decided about what happens to the leaders?"

I nod. "Have you made up your mind?"

Her mouth twists. "No. I don't... I'm not sure what the right way is."

"It's a lot of responsibility." I should know. I make these decisions day in, day out. A rival, a retaliation, an enemy. All their lives in my palm. Anything that keeps Jeanette happy and away from those who mean her harm is a no-brainer to me, so I hadn't even thought about letting the Carters and Fletchers live. But she hasn't had this weight on her shoulders before. Does she really even want it? "If you don't want blood on your hands, I'll send you to a new safe house without knowing what happened. You can leave at midnight, as we originally agreed."

That makes her gaze snap to mine. "No! If you'll allow me, I want to make the judgement. Can you hold off on the safe house and the... Permanent solution... Until I've made my mind up?"

"Yes." It's good she's thinking about this seriously. And there's another reason to be happy about her indecision. Every hour she isn't sure if she wants escape or blood, she remains with me. "You have all the time you need."

A secret smile lights her eyes, so subtle that anyone who didn't study her as hard as I do wouldn't notice it.

"What would you like to do today?" I ask.

"I get a choice?" she scoffs.

"I aim to please my prisoner." She has no idea how much.

"More lessons on defence." Her chin tilts up.

"Okay." I like the idea of protecting her myself, of course. But if defending herself is what she needs, I'll provide. "You know what your two best securities are?"

She narrows her eyes as she thinks. "A gun. And a knife."

I laugh, I can't help it. She's a true innocent.

"What?" She scowls and it's adorable. Like a grumpy kitten. I want to scoop her up and kiss the pucker from between her graceful brows.

"Instinct. That tingle in your spine and the back of your mind. The knowledge your body has that something is wrong. That's your best shield from danger." It's all very well for me to feel that tingle and smile with anticipation of the ignorant arses I'll scrub from the world. But I want her to be cautious. She is more precious than a dozen Fabergé eggs. She's priceless and irreplaceable.

Her forehead wrinkles and I reach over to stroke the lines away. "I'll take care of you as long as you're here. And after that, your words, beautiful girl. Your wit and your insight. Keep him talking."

"I've never been much good at that." Fiddling with the hem of her top, she crosses and uncrosses her legs, drawing my gaze. They're long and slim and a little coltish. Like she's still learning how they work, and how the brush of her thighs together can affect a man. "Talking, I mean. I always say the wrong thing, and people misunderstand me."

"Me too," I confess without thinking. All my thoughts are with her lovely calves.

"The big mafia boss is misunderstood." She tilts her head and skims her gaze over me. I suddenly fear maybe she can see everything, including how gone I am for her. "You're terrifying and brutal. You killed a man without a second glance yesterday."

I open my mouth to say the shot was to the shoulder, to incapacitate not kill, and I told my second-in-command to clean up. Linda knows to save a life if possible. But Jeanette continues. "You're the playboy kingpin. You're a ruthless businessman. A cliche in a smart suit with a glass of expensive alcohol and a penthouse suite of ten floors in the most prestigious address in London."

I nod, but honestly, I'm a little disappointed. Yes, I am all of those things.

"But I suppose you are misunderstood. Because you're also kind and do what you think is right, despite the consequences. You looked after me even though you didn't need to and I *told you not to*, and started a war within your mafia alliance for a slip of a girl—"

"You're not just a slip of a girl," I mutter.

"You're hardworking—don't think I didn't see your laptop open last night—and you look after your people. You're never seen with the same woman on your arm twice, which means you don't cruelly raise hopes. And I think..." She pauses and licks her lips. It's a guileless gesture, probably indicating her nerves, but it sizzles down my back. "I think you're lonely."

My lungs collapse. So does my heart. Every one of my internal organs throws down tools and shrugs with a, *she's got you, boss*. Not even a full day we've spent together as adults and it's like she's not just *in* my thoughts, she can *pick through* my thoughts.

How does she know all that?

"Apparently I'm not misunderstood by you." This girl sees straight into my soul.

"Takes one to know one," she mumbles, and looks away, suddenly shy.

No parents to love and encourage her, a traumatic past she must hide from everyone, and a starchy private school. I can see why she's lonely too. She needs someone who knows her and cares for her without end. Someone who loves her to the outermost stars that look black from here on earth, and back again.

Like me.

And that care means not pushing her further right now. "Very perceptive. What about we try some more practical scenarios. Self-defence *only*," I add.

Gratitude flares in her eyes when she looks up and agrees with a soft, "Okay."

Back in the gym, there's a tacit agreement that we're to be serious. I spend hours ignoring my body's reaction to hers when I grab her, again and again, from different angles and in various ways and congratulate her as I wince when she ultimately manages to land some hits. I teach her how to listen to my breathing and predict which direction I'm going to lunge. She's whip-smart and picks up everything after one or two goes.

Eventually, she flops onto the springy rubber mat and groans. Her top rides up a little and I avert my gaze.

"I'm knackered."

"That was nothing compared to being in my bed," I say under my breath. Not low enough for her to miss, however. She perks up.

"Sit down with me." Patting the space next to her, she gets this sexy, excited smile on her face.

"Jeanette," I warn, but as I fold my long limbs onto the floor mats at a decent distance, my knees creaking.

"What about from this angle," she chirps with false innocence. She knows exactly what she's doing as she scoots across to me. "We haven't practised on the ground. Or what if I was on a bed?"

"You're not going to be on the floor with a man. And *definitely* not a bed." That comes out rather more like a decree than I intend, but I've had to keep my arousal on a leash as tight and stretched as elastic, and I can't promise I won't break if she tests me.

"You said to exploit sensitive areas." Her hand is tentative as she reaches down. I hold my breath, unable to think or feel or rationalise the myriad of reasons I should put a stop to this.

My desire for this girl has turned me inside out. She makes me into a monster who would snatch her away and covet her for himself.

"What if..." She shuffles closer on her knees. With her hair spilling out from the braid and over her shoulders she's my daydreams come to life. Her small hands grip the waistband of my shorts and her mouth opens in a gasp as she drags them down, revealing my rock-solid erection.

For a second I'm convinced she'll take one look at my big cock and run away. But although she blushes furiously, she doesn't back down. My brave girl.

"It does look sensitive. This vein..." She traces a featherlight trail down my length.

I should stop her. I should pull up my shorts and return us to what we were doing. But I can't do anything but stare.

"Would this be an effective way of fighting you off?" she says teasingly, but before I can choke a reply her lips cover my cock. Tentatively at first, unsure of how to proceed, but the feel of her warm wet mouth has me unable to move.

"Of incapacitating me," I groan. "Temporarily."

She kisses over the head of my cock, her lips shiny with my precum.

Another man whispers, "Take it into your mouth." Not me. I wouldn't encourage this when I know it's only escalating my obsession with her.

She sucks me and my hips jerk involuntarily. I'm crazy with the feel of her wet lips.

"But it's not a good ploy." I growl the advice out against every instinct in me, all of which want her to continue.

"Mmm?" Her enquiring noise hums through the sensitive end of my cock and it's all I can do not to come there and then.

"I suspect you're going to be very, very good at this. If your aim is to escape, it's a disaster. I might never let you go." A warning and a promise, but she purrs with contentment. "And if you try this on any other man but me I'd have to kill him."

That makes her shake with silent laughter, but she doesn't stop moving over my cock.

"Not a joke," I grind out. Jeanette belongs to me. Nothing would keep me from protecting her. The only force in the universe that will prevent me from claiming her is *her*. She could leave me, accept the safe house I've offered and I'd be a shell of a man, half a person, empty and dead. But I'd still look after her and I'd still do my duty like a massive oak tree, hollow on the inside but sustaining life.

One thing matters to me and I'd burn this city to the ground if that was what was needed to make her happy.

Her violet eyes are full of wonder when they meet mine. She fidgets her legs as she works her mouth on my cock, pressing them together and circling her hips. And I think... Damn but I think this turns her on.

But though part of me is desperate to flip this and satisfy the ache she must have between her legs, the little noises she's making and the rhythm of her bobbing onto my cock are like a drug. I give in to her. I lean back and allow myself to watch her glossy lips take me.

I've imagined this as I've jerked off into my hand too many times to admit, but the reality is even better. It's just as filthy, but it's heart-wrenchingly tender as well. Her hair tickles my inner thigh and she might not have done this before but that's part of her appeal. She doesn't know to completely cover her teeth and it's the tiny sensations that make this more than my imagination could have conjured. The brush of her hair. The occasional jab of slight pain as she catches me only heightens the pleasure. And the way she's enjoying it too, that's what slays me. Her pebbled nipples showing through her top.

I store every detail away. I don't close my eyes and just feel. I observe her intensely. For this moment, she's my only thought. I'm her captor, her watcher, her guard. Nothing she does will go unnoticed by me.

It takes all my strength not to grab the back of her head, or tangle my fingers in her hair. Another time, I promise myself, even though I know that's a promise I'll break. I would love to unleash a bit of violence and fuck her mouth, but she's sweet in her exploration. I let her suck me. That was the point, after all, of my teaching her self-defence—so she could feel strong. Looking down at her, I can see that in spadefuls. She knows I'm losing my mind, and is enjoying every second of my capitulation.

And much as I want to draw this out, as I want to spend the rest of my life with Jeanette knelt between my knees with my cock in her mouth, I feel it building, threatening and inevitable as day turning to night.

"I'm going to come," I warn her.

And the minx, I swear she smiles. Her eyes light up and where I thought she liked the feeling of power, I see she's *relishing* it.

Even as her inexperienced ministrations tip me over into orgasm, I don't close my eyes. I keep watching her every tiny expression. I'm never going to forget even one second of this one day when I was lucky enough to have Jeanette Capelle, and she took my soul.

I see her surprise the moment my seed hits the back of her throat and fills her mouth. I'm nearly undone by her slow smile as she tastes me and then swallows every drop. She feels naughty doing that, and fuck, but so do I. Defiling my girl like this.

Before my cock has stopped twitching and pulsing, I reach and grab her under her slight arms, dragging her up my body to kiss her. My cock is lewdly pressed between our clothes, and she stiffens in alarm before melting into me as I thread my fingers into her hair as I always wanted to, and press our mouths together.

A sweet kiss. Our first real kiss. Gentle and delicate after the intensity of what we've done. I breathe in her honey and rose scent and try to tell her with my kiss all the words I dare not say aloud.

I love you.

I can't let you go.

You're mine.

Then I hold her tight as I flip her onto her back and slide down her body. The understanding between us is so pure, she knows what I'm going to do. She wriggles out of her jeans and knickers and fuck, when she spreads her legs wide with only a touch from my hands to push her knees apart, I fall on her.

There's no pretence. I lick her like I'm starving. I might have just come, but my need for her is undiminished. I'm merciless in the pursuit of her quaking under my tongue. I feast and I'm not easy on her. I use my fingers, curling them into her passage and pistoning them in and out. She's soaking wet, dripping with need and I push her without stopping, hard and harder on that little bud, listening to her moans and cries. I band my arm over her pelvis when she starts to shake, holding her down. I won't let her escape even one bit of the pleasure I'm going to overwhelm her with.

It doesn't take long and my chest expands with satisfaction when I feel her clench around the fingers I'm thrusting into her. When I think of how this is a first for her I'm hard again.

Afterwards, I carry her to my bathroom. It's a herculean effort when we're both under the sluicing hot water, soapy and clean and wet, not to do anything but worship her breasts with my mouth and make her come again on my fingers. The roar of my achingly hard cock is as unrelenting as the water.

I ignore it. And though she casts curious eyes down at my erection, she doesn't object when I guide her hand from me. But she looks at me like I'm a puzzle she's trying to figure out. I don't know how many times I can cope with coming with her until I'll snap and demand entrance to her pussy. Or just take it.

I feed her—thankfully my amazing housekeeper left

plenty of meals in the fridge. Jeanette oohs over everything she finds and spends ten straight minutes dithering between her two favourites. She says it's a Libra thing. I tell her it's an Aries thing that she should just have both, and she laughs. I stand behind her with my hands on her hips as she decides.

I don't remind her of the other decision she needs to make. If two lunch options consume so much of her time, how will she ever choose about the fate of living, breathing, people?

We decide on a film for the afternoon, and she cuddles into me on the sofa like *I'm* her favourite armchair. It's a thriller with a heavy dollop of romance, and I pause the film when there's a gun on screen and explain how to remove the safety and the recoil to expect when it fires. An acknowledgement of the continued teacher role I promised her.

She's silent for a while. It's all too easy to kid myself this is a normal weekend for us. This is what we do, her and me. Give each other orgasms and stick together like a mated pair.

I assume she's forgotten about the truths she wanted as well as the help with fighting off threats. Until she says that a scene in the film reminds her of her school, and I reply that, yes, it looks like Switzerland and she suddenly sits up, snatches the remote and the screen goes black.

Her eyebrows pinch together.

"How do you know I was at school in Switzerland? I was the *lost princess*."

8

JEANETTE

He scowls. "Do you really want to hear this?"

My stomach dips with disappointment. I was beginning to think I could trust him to tell me straight and not like a child.

"Now," I snap. There isn't long left. At midnight the day we bargained for is up, and then the moment I tell him my decision about what to do with his enemies, I'm free to go.

Funnily enough, I'm finding that an impossible choice to make, or even think about.

"I never lost you."

I blink in surprise.

"I always knew where you were. To me, you were never lost."

"What?" That should scare me but instead his words spread heat across my back like a perfectly cosy warm seat to nestle in. One that brackets me on all sides, safe and protected.

I was never lost.

The comfort is irrational. It can't change the way I felt

at the time: alone. Betrayed by every friend and all my family when I realised how they had used me. But it makes no sense. "The police told me no one knew where I was, and there was a fund for protective custody."

"There was." He circles his hand and smiles wryly, but it doesn't reach his eyes. "I provided it."

"How?" I can't process this. "When did it start? Actually, no. All the way back. Tell me exactly what happened after..." After I was drugged.

"You really want to recall this? It's not pretty, angel."

I nod. All I've ever known was a blur like a video that wouldn't stream properly.

"By the time I heard, you were already married. I arrived at the Fletcher compound. Suffice to say he wasn't pleased to see me and there was a disagreement. He was intent on having his wedding night, despite you being unconscious. I couldn't let that happen. I had to remove you by force, and a number on both sides didn't make it home that night. I took you to hospital and told them to call the police."

It was him. I never knew. All these years, I just woke up from a horrible nightmarish dream, but I'd never known who had fetched me out. And it was Sebastian.

"Then I organised your annulment. Your education. Your protection. And every year I received an update on you. On your birthday."

He has watched me since. All those days when I was sad and had no one, he was watching.

But he could have been in my life.

"Why didn't you contact me? Every birthday? Could have sent a card," I say with false lightness.

"Would you have welcomed that?"

I consider. A reminder of all that had been taken from me? "No. But still. Didn't you want to?"

He hesitates.

"No lies," I add.

"Yes and no."

"I'm the Libra, weighing everything up constantly, not you." I spread my hands as if to grip his neck in frustration. "I might yet throttle you."

He smiles in recollection at our spat last night, but breathes in like the cares of the world are on his back.

"On your seventeenth birthday, I was sick to my stomach. You looked dead inside and out. I thought we'd screwed you up permanently. I didn't want to contact you." His words spill out, fast and unflinching and truthful as scalding water poured from a kettle. "Eighteen, you were a little better. I wanted to hug you and muzz your hair like you were my little sister."

Like we were family. I wish I'd known. Those years... I'd left everything familiar behind and struggled to understand people. I thought I'd been totally deserted. But I hadn't. He'd searched for clues in a report, while I'd been staring at the sky.

"Nineteen. You looked happy. I was delighted. I stared at that photo and told myself it was okay. You'd survived. I hadn't failed you as badly as I thought. I kept it framed on my desk that whole year. You'd got the hang of dying your hair and it looked good. I saw that you were due to get straight As at school. You still wore that uniform but there was a confidence I hadn't seen before. And I was proud as fuck of you for making it through.

"Then twenty." He swallows. "You were self-assured. The first photograph of you not in a school uniform. You wore a pale blue summer dress."

I remember it. That was my favourite and I wore it constantly.

He shrugs. "It was a far cry from a blouse buttoned to your neck and a shapeless blazer. You were on the cusp of womanhood. And I... I responded with a man's urges. I saw you and I burned. I wanted. I desired.

"And I knew, without a shadow of doubt, that I could never have you. That I would not drag you back to this life you'd escaped. I took down the sweet photo of you from the year before. I couldn't trust myself to look at it and not imagine what you looked like now. And I couldn't trust myself not to give in to the soul deep longing for you to be mine."

There's a silence.

I think of seeing newspaper columns about playboy bachelor Sebastian Laurent. I think of how I yearned for him to be my husband, my protector, my companion and my lover. How would I have felt, knowing it was mutual?

Excited. Hopeful. With a whole life to look forward to rather than an awkward feeling of needing to escape the inevitability of being trapped, desperate to know what the future had in store and willing to use anything—including balls of gas billions of light years away—to try to understand myself, my situation, and my fate.

"Do you still... Want that?" I ask cautiously. "Me?"

His eyes are harshly bright, like looking at the midday sun on an alpine glacier—all the heat and light reflected onto every inch of my body. I've never had anyone look at me the way Sebastian does. That intensity is both scary and thrilling.

"More."

He's like a crouched jaguar, ready to pounce, but

somehow I know after his confession he's not going to make the first move. I have to do that.

I screw up my courage. He says he wants this. I can tempt him into taking me, right? This should be simple; it should have been straightforward from the beginning, except we both naffed it up at almost every turn.

What would a sexy, experienced woman do?

Ugh. I don't even know. And maybe that doesn't matter. I crawl over the sofa until I'm on him. I'm a little awkward, unsure of our strange mess of limbs, and he hasn't reached out to touch me.

Not bloody giving me any help at all. So typical of Sebastian. When it's what he's decided, there's no stopping him, but until then, I'm on my own. And yet, I'm not. His looking out for me, his caring for me, everything he's done to ensure my comfort and safety, it's this massive net to catch me whenever I fall.

So I jump.

Metaphorically. For the main part. I lunge into his lap and press my mouth inexpertly to his. But he's not responding. He's holding himself like a granite statue.

"I want you too," I say between kisses, trying to get him to join in. I reach for the buttons of his shirt and he grasps my wrists and holds them away from him.

Does he not want me? Maybe he meant "more" as in, *oh that was such a little aspiration to just have you, now I want that supermodel from last night*. I thought he meant that he wanted me *more* now, but perhaps I was wrong. Fear deflates me and I stop.

But then I recall the agony of discipline and desire in his eyes earlier. "I'm your captive, remember?" I twist my fingers to stroke his knuckles.

Sebastian releases my wrists, but instead of pulling me

to him as I expect, he grabs my hair and tugs my head back, making me gasp. His grey eyes spear me.

"Don't tease," he grinds out. "I'll only be pushed so far."

"I'm not teasing. I want to be yours." The snag of pain from my hair being pulled is slight but enough to sensitise all my skin, as though every nerve is connected.

"Angel." He brings our heads close together, then dips his and breathes in the scent of my neck. He closes his eyes and lines crease his cheeks like it hurts him. "If I have you once, I won't let you go. If you allow me to join our bodies, to thrust into your virgin pussy, I won't stop there. You'll be *mine*. I'll claim you. That freedom you wanted? Gone. You'd be here, as my queen, by my side."

His chin tilts up and he tightens his grip on my hair. I can tell he means this, and perhaps intends to terrify me. To make me think twice.

"But I'd have *you*."

"You'll have my heart forever, wherever you are." He still hasn't touched my skin, holding me away. "But yes, if you wanted me in your life, to have, to hold..." He stops as though his mouth ran away with him and he didn't mean to invoke marriage vows. Then he seems to accept it and continues. "To orgasm on my tongue and my cock every day and every night. To be loved and adored. Yes, angel. You'd have *me* if you go through with what I see in your eyes. But I want you to be really certain. Because if I take your virginity, I won't let you go."

"Yes. Yes to all of that." I've never been more sure about anything in my whole life. I was born a mafia princess; I will live as a queen. My place in the world is by Sebastian's side.

He lets out a half growl, half groan and buries his face in my neck, pulling me flush to him.

"We'll need a bed." His arms wrap around my waist and

I squeak as he stands. "Because though I will happily have you bounce on my cock on the sofa, and take you from behind against that big window, and any and all of the filthy-hot things we could do, the first time will be comfortable. You're going to be under me and I'm going to make it so good you won't stop shaking for a week."

"Yes." I'd be happy with any of the ways he mentioned, and I don't doubt we'll get around to all of them. But I don't care so long as it's Sebastian and me.

He kicks open the bedroom door and lays me on the bed. I only have eyes for him. And now I've unleashed him, he's intent on undressing me. I try to get to the button of his shirt but he bats my hands away to unzip my dress and push it down. I help, lifting my bottom and he makes a sound of approval from the back of his throat when he sees the underwear I put on after the shower.

White lace. Matching.

It's pretty and feminine. No underwire on the bra—my little breasts never need it—and the soft fabric has caressed my skin all day.

"I thought you'd like this set." I pluck at the strap of the bra and give him a teasing smile.

"Angel, I love it. So forgive me." He rears up, takes either side of the bra in his fists and tears it in two.

My eyes must be the size of dinner plates as he reaches deliberately down and grips the knickers the same way.

"Because pretty as this is, it isn't your naked skin. And I can't wait another moment to see all of you."

For a second the fabric bites into my flesh, but then the sound of ripping rents the air. I gasp, but partly it's not the shock. It's how instantly hot and achy I am between the legs from how impatient he is to see all of me. And I'm the same about him.

"I can't rip your clothes," I say, shoving at his clothes. "Undress for me." Not just the partial views of his chest or his cock. I'm eager too.

Big and powerful and dangerous as he is, he laughs softly at my bossy demand, but obeys. He strips so quickly I almost ask him to do it again. Instead, I reach for him, smoothing my hands over his shoulders and chest. I explore his upper arms and he lets me, watching me discover him. They're covered in scars, some round, others long and curved, that I trace with my fingertips and my throat closes with gratitude that none of these wounds prevented him from being here with me now. Then I slip back to the "V" of muscles at his hips and further to that intriguing silky hardness that somehow is miraculously supposed to fit into me.

"Nope." He removes my hands from his cock. "You're going to lie there and take what I give you, Jeanette," he purrs my name like he loves saying it. And in his voice the name that usually represents how alone I am sounds like home.

You were never lost to me.

He covers me with his body, all heat and smooth solid planes of his chest and hair that's softer than I imagined. His elbows are planted each side of my shoulders and he cradles my face in his hands as he kisses me. Sweetly, then deeper, angling his lips on mine and his tongue demanding entry. I open my mouth and the throbbing need at my core intensifies.

Aligning us so his cock notches between my legs, he groans. I feel his cock, hot and hard at my entrance. Impossibly thick. There is no way that monster is going inside me, and yet, there is no way I'm going anywhere until I'm impaled on him. He feels far too blunt to split me open, but I'm desperate and wet and my pussy is clenching with need.

However much it hurts, I don't care. It will be sore in all the best ways and I will love every second.

His lips brush mine. "I love you."

I don't get a chance for my brain to register that, or respond because the first push of his body into mine makes me gasp. There's a pinch.

"Relax," he croons and strokes down my chest, rubbing over one nipple. "If you're not relaxed enough to come on my cock within five minutes, I swear I'll spank you until you learn to take me without trying to cut off my blood supply."

I splutter with laughter and probably it's that which eases all my muscles and the twinge of pain is gone. I feel Sebastian's smile against my lips.

"Good girl." He pushes deeper. And this time it's a moan of pleasure at the slide of him, and the stretch.

He withdraws just a little and I grasp ineffectually to bring him back. Then he's further inside of me and I arch into him, trusting him to do this right. I touch the soles of my feet together around his waist and cling to his neck.

When he pushes all the way in on the next thrust there's nothing like it in my life before. I've never been this close to anyone. There's nothing between us, just sheer love and honesty in his silver eyes. It's him and me and we're almost the same thing. I wriggle and dig my heels into his back until I'm even more open to him, until we're flush together and my clit is pressed to his skin, and he stills, letting me accustom myself to being filled by him.

In that moment I know, without a shadow of a doubt, that he's mine and I'm his, and it would take a clash of galaxies to drag us apart.

"Angel." He kisses me softly, and traces his fingers down my thigh. "I have to move. You feel too good, and I promise you there's more for you. But I swear if I don't thrust into you, I'm going to die."

I giggle again, and loosen my grip on his waist. Then he's easing in and out of me, and oh god I now know why everyone makes a fuss about sex. Having him deep was wonderful but this is even more. He's stroking me from the inside out.

My hips sync up with his thrusts without conscious thought.

And the pleasure begins to build.

9

SEBASTIAN

I'm her first.

It shouldn't matter, and I'd love her the same if I wasn't, but knowing I'm the one to take her innocence gives me savage pride. It gives me a masculine thrill so primal I can barely acknowledge it to myself.

"Mine," I growl into her neck. Softly. I'm not sure my girl is ready to hear that I'm so possessive of her. But she is *mine*. I won't let her go. She's given herself to me and honestly, all I want is to claim her again and again until she's so replete with pleasure she won't ever think of being anywhere but by my side.

"Yours," she whispers so gently I'm not certain I heard her correctly.

I thrust in and out of her sweet tight hole, trying to be careful, but she's arching into me, urging me on. Her arms around my shoulders, nails digging into my back. If my little wildcat claws me as she comes I'd wear those scars with more pride than any of the ones from fights.

"Sebastian," she moans my name and that goes straight to my cock.

"Tell me," I demand. "Tell me how my thick cock feels in your little virgin pussy, Jeanette."

She whimpers and tightens around me and I almost laugh. Oh she likes that does she?

"Tell me how it feels to be taken by the man who waited for you. Who always was meant to have you."

"Yes," she moans. "It was always you. I just didn't realise, couldn't see how we were always the right fit."

And fit we do. Perfectly. I adjust the angle so I'm thrusting deeper, and it's entirely different to the slow slide I made as I first entered her and took her virginity. Controlled still, but more intense. Faster and more.

"I'm going to fill you up, angel. I want to put a baby in you."

Shit. That slipped out. But I can't take it back and I won't.

There's a heartbeat of time when I think this is all over and I've fucked up and this will all stop. She'll say it's all too fast and there'll be more waiting or maybe she'll decide I'm too obsessed with her.

The air is thick honey, suffocatingly sweet. This pleasure might kill me if I can't have it again. If Jeanette doesn't want the same things I do, if she doesn't choose forever this might be my end.

Her heels find my buttocks and her legs cross at my waist and she's pulling me to her.

"Yes. Yes, more."

She clenches around my length and goddamn I can breathe again. And it wasn't like I stopped, but the energy that flows through me now is molten gold.

"Make me yours in every way."

I give in.

One second I'm being careful, the next, I'm grasping her hip and thrusting into her hard and fast.

"This is mine," I tell her. "No man will ever touch you, or do this to you. I'll destroy anyone who tries. You are all fucking mine, and I'll mark you with my come every day, so you can't forget."

She whines and I feel her nod, her lips moving against mine in acceptance. My blood roars.

I pound her into the mattress, holding nothing back. There is only her and me, joined.

Inside her. Where I'm meant to be. The slide of our bodies together is a magic unlike anything I've ever felt and I have to make her come, because I can't hold out. I'm going to come inside her, fill her with my seed, and it's impossible to stop.

I reach between us and the moment my fingers stroke her clit she shudders and cries out, pulsing around my cock. I don't know whether it's the sound of her pleasure ringing in my ears or the feel of her coming on my cock that sends me over, but I'm coming with her, pushed by the knowledge I've satisfied my girl.

It's all-encompassing. I'm wracked, emptying myself into her. She grips me everywhere throughout. My cock, waist, shoulders. Like she'll never let me go.

The pleasure of her body is only half of it though. Yes, being with Jeanette is like finding the broken edges of myself slot perfectly with hers. Yes, she's unutterably beautiful and I want her to come on my cock time after time. I want to feel her tipping me into orgasm. But as the shocks of coming ease, it's my heart that doesn't recover.

I'm gone for her like a black hole is gone for light. I'll gobble up every part of Jeanette she'll allow me to have. I'll give and take pleasure with her until there's nothing left of either of us but stardust and longing.

I kiss her throat, I rub my cheek against her jaw. I gently nip her ear and when she giggles and tries to pull me closer, even though I'm lying on top of her. She struggles to get me to rest my full weight on her, and I protest that I'll crush her.

She holds me to her anyway.

Trapping her slight body under mine is better than it ought to be.

10

JEANETTE

I have never slept in a bed this comfortable, or with a blanket this perfectly warm.

But wait.

There's a brush of movement.

The blanket is Sebastian's arm and his chest behind me. Sebastian is kissing my neck, his arm around my waist. Everything from yesterday rushes back.

I'm not alone anymore.

He promised forever last night, and this morning he still wants me. He's whispering words about how beautiful I am. How I'm his, and he's mine, and he can't wait for us to have babies together. There're smutty words too, about how much he wants me, how every perfect part of my body was made for him.

By the time I'm wild and wailing with need, he allows me to turn in his arms. Then he's cupping my bottom and sliding me onto his cock as we both moan with the rightness of it. Impossibly, this feels even better than last night. Without the twinge of discomfort there's just the pleasure of him stretching me out.

And Sebastian is both rougher, more impatient, and more tender this time. He pulls me close, our fronts touching all the way down and never lets up his kiss except to murmur filthy words of love and need. But at the same time, he's not holding back, thrusting into me hard, holding me tightly. And I love it. I cling to him and take everything he gives.

"You better come quickly," he growls when I'm mind-less with the feel of him inside me. "Your tight pussy is going to tip me over. But I won't come until you do."

"I..." I'm nothing but his to do with as he likes, and to do as he says. And since he tells me to come and shifts the angle to press onto my clit as he pounds into me, I do.

"Good girl."

Those words make a fresh wave of orgasm engulf me and Sebastian gives one last hard thrust and then is shaking as he comes too. Inside me, filling me up. In that moment and the long minutes afterwards when he doesn't let me go, softly kissing and nipping my lips, I think we might have permanently fused together. I've never felt so loved and cared for in my life.

"Right." Sebastian rolls onto his back and takes me with him, and gets to his feet.

I squeak.

"I've got you."

And it's only when we're standing under the shower that he finally slides out of me. I give an unwitting noise of dissent and Sebastian chuckles.

"Yes, again, soon."

I pout as he piles my hair on top of my head and brings one of my hands to hold it while he washes my back in indulgent sweeps of his palms.

"I miss you."

"I'm right here." He kisses the sensitive spot where my hair meets my neck.

"I miss you *down there*." And I feel oh-so-daring.

"My greedy girl." His hand lingers lower, over my arse, then traces around and cups my pussy.

Somewhere, far away, a phone rings.

"Ignore it," Sebastian directs as he slides his fingers into my folds.

Sebastian has fresh coffee and pastries ready in the kitchen by the time I finish in the shower. He smiles when he sees me wearing his shirt.

"All those clothes I bought you, and you prefer this?" He takes advantage of the gaping hem to stroke the backs of my thighs as he kisses me.

I'm boosted onto the stool of the kitchen island and he watches like a panther as I choose a pain au chocolat. A low growl and he piles a cinnamon roll and a croissant onto my plate.

"Need to keep your energy up even more now you might be pregnant," he replies when I shoot him a look.

The trill of a phone cuts into the cosy domesticity of our breakfast and Sebastian scowls as he checks the screen.

"It's alright. Answer it." He's put his life on hold for me, but I know he has responsibilities. "I need to check in with my boss anyway."

"We'll talk about that." A kiss to my cheek, then he snaps into a ruthless mafia kingpin rather than my Sebastian. "This better be important."

I try not to listen as he speaks, but my stomach drops.

There's something wrong. He sighs and when he returns he's rubbing his forehead. Bumping my knees apart, he takes my chin in his finger and thumb and tilts my face until I'm looking into his eyes.

"If I leave to manage a problem, will you promise to stay here, and still be my sweet happy girl when I return?" He's staring at me with hope and fear. "Ross is causing chaos, wrecking shops and throwing out all sorts of claims, challenging me to a duel. He won't go without me turning up to deal with it, or so he says. My people need me, but I need you safe. Don't leave." He says it as an order, but I don't mind. Maybe I even quite like it...

"Be careful." There's a tickle in my mind that this is a trap they're laying for him.

"Angel, I will always come home to you."

"Yes." Every day I'll choose him.

He strokes my cheek. "I'll be back as soon as I can."

The apartment is quiet without him. I watch a bit of TV, but can't help being distracted by what could have been serious enough to drag him away.

It's only after he's been gone an hour that I realise there's a landline. I could call my boss on my mobile phone and explain.

"Darling!" She picks up within one ring. "Are you feeling better?"

Ooop. I'd forgotten I was supposed to be ill.

"Yeah," I cough. "Much better, thanks." Multiple orgasms will do that to a person. As will finding the love of my life.

"Are you well enough to see me?" she says hopefully. "I desperately need your help getting a new chart reading onto Face-thingy."

"Of course!" I say before I can stop myself. I want this

job, but I promised Sebastian... "Can it wait until tomorrow?"

"It *must* be today. You know how time sensitive these readings are. And my audience has already missed out for a whole day. We'll lose momentum. Isn't that what you said?"

It is. But I can't... I really mustn't...

But neither can I allow myself to lose this job. Whatever Sebastian said about me running my own business, I've worked hard to get Priscilla to where she is, and I can't ditch her. I haven't quit just because I took one sick day.

"Can you come here?" Because while I want to keep my job, I'm not a complete idiot. Sebastian told me to stay, I agreed, and I meant it. I won't cross London looking for trouble.

There's a pause before she agrees, and I wonder what it means. Probably that she doesn't want to pack up her charts. I give her the address I find on junk mail and she says she'll be twenty minutes.

Just enough time to put on some proper clothes. After a bit of dithering, I choose a pale blue skater dress amongst the clothing Sebastian bought for me and smile at the way it echoes the dress I loved a couple of summers ago, but has expensive details that make it grown up. The fabric is light and silky and it floats over my body like a dream.

The phone ringing jerks me out of a fantasy about what Sebastian will do when he sees me wearing the dress. It's Priscilla.

"Jeanette, I can get this lift to work. Can you come down to the basement car park?"

I sigh internally. This is peak Priscilla. She really is terrible with technology. I'm not the best, but even I can post on social media and use an elevator. I think about telling her to take the stairs, but honestly that's a bit mean. We must be forty floors up.

"Sure. I'll be right down." I'm not leaving the building, so I'm hardly breaking my word to Sebastian.

A trickle of unease goes down my back as I step into the lift. I am technically Sebastian's captive. Maybe he has done something so I can't escape?

But the buttons respond to my touch and though I should feel relief, the apprehension remains. It's just that it's a fast drop, I tell myself as the doors slide open and reveal a silent car park. Nothing more than that.

"Hello!" I emerge and look to right and left, but Priscilla is nowhere to be seen.

Huh.

A car door opens and Priscilla gets out. "Oh thank god you're here. Come and do this for me. I'm lost without you." She smiles but it's a bit... Sickly.

"Are you alright?" Something is odd, like a spot the difference image. I can't see what isn't as it should be.

I take a step towards Priscilla.

"Oh yes, I'm fine." She doesn't sound fine. "Just typical Pisces problems."

My heart stops.

Because Priscilla isn't a Pisces. She's a Sagittarius sun sign with moon in Taurus.

"Priscilla, what's going on?"

"I've come for you, princess." Ross Fletcher's voice comes from right behind me and I'm shaking with fear, real terror utterly unlike what I ever felt when practising with Sebastian.

No. This is fear of endless cold black holes and hissing red eyes. It's dread of ancient evil like the freezing space between stars.

When he grabs me by the wrist, I act instinctively, all the work with Sebastian paying off. My head jerks back and cracks on his chin with a sickening bang that shoots pain through my skull too.

"Fuck!" But he doesn't let me go. He tightens his grip even as I twist... the wrong way. "You are coming with me," he hisses. "I'm having what you denied me, wife."

"No!" I'm not being taken by that monster.

I kick out in panic and hit his leg. The force of my kick unbalances me. I crumple to the floor and something clatters as he swears again. Pain flares on my hip where I hit the concrete.

He's still got me though, and as I look up. I know it's useless.

There's a roar in my ears, in my head. Grey noise I can't decipher.

I'm going to be right back to where I was at sixteen. In this evil man's power, helpless, and *alone*. Deserted by all my friends and family. And this time, Sebastian won't be able to save me, because he's across the city helping others, assuming I'm snug and secure.

"No you don't," Fletcher snaps and leans down, reaching for my hair. And I see it. His gun, that's what clattered to the ground with me. Not even thinking I throw myself across and snatch it up. My thumb finds the safety— as Sebastian taught me—and I press the trigger without aiming or considering, just *at him*. Because I *cannot* go with him.

Ross screams and releases my wrist and hair as he falls to the floor beside me, clutching his thigh. It's spurting red.

I shot him. My mind is blunt with shock. He was going to hurt me, and instead I shot him.

"Jeanette!"

I can't look away from what I've done. I'm stone. Unable to move. There's blood everywhere, a veritable fountain that Fletcher uselessly has his palm over.

"Angel." Strong arms lift me and I'm brittle, cracking as I curl into Sebastian's embrace.

"You came." The relief to be back with Sebastian is like the clouds parting on a dark night to reveal the moon. He doesn't negate everything bad, but he guilds it all in pretty silver, making it impossible to be scared anymore. There's not the harsh light of day. There's enough.

"Always. Always." He strokes my hair and I hide my face in his shirt and breathe in the sandalwood and citrus scent of him. "I knew something was wrong as soon as I arrived, and after I ..."

"Did you..." I find the ground with my feet and grab Sebastian's arm as I look into his face. And I see the truth in the hard set of his jaw. He killed my father because he deserved it. And because he wanted to protect me.

"Jeanette, I'm sorry. I had to make the choice for you."

I should feel regret, but I don't. I only feel glad. Did my father die quickly or slowly and quietly like Fletcher? For all I have longed for family love, it doesn't matter now.

Because I have Sebastian, and he is everything I didn't know I needed.

There's a gurgle from the floor. I made a choice too and I glance down. The fountain is already a little stream. Sebastian follows my gaze and I feel him tense.

"Is it safe?" my boss pipes up. It takes me a moment to see her, crouched behind a car.

"For now," Sebastian all but snarls, his temper flicking like a switch. "Leave before I change my mind. And find a new administrative assistant."

"It wasn't her fault—" I start to protest, but Sebastian slaps my arse, hard. I suppress a yelp and glare at him.

"You liked it," he murmurs into my hair, and I can't deny that. The sting of his hand on my buttocks has sent an inappropriate bolt of need between my legs.

Moments later, there's the clip of Priscilla's shoes as she runs from the car park.

"Good luck!" I call after her, then turn to chide Sebastian softly. "Was it necessary to scare her?"

"I'm letting her go, aren't I?" He shrugs. "No one gets to be around you but those who would lay down their lives for you. That's my rule. She led him here."

We both look down at Fletcher. He's still.

"Sorry," I whisper with a twinge of guilt, though I know he can't hear me anymore.

"That bullet hit an artery; it wasn't your fault. But from the moment he touched you, he was a dead man." Sebastian squeezes my waist possessively and leads me to the elevator. "He's lucky you got to him before I did. My way would have been far more painful."

And I know, without a shadow of a doubt, that Sebastian will always protect me. He doesn't care about anyone but me. His only regret is that I killed that bastard and he didn't. I'm certain as he lifts me by the rump and presses me against the glass, kissing me hungrily, that he'd do anything. Great and terrible things to look after me. No longer the lost princess, I am his Queen. When the doors open, he doesn't put me down, striding straight through to his blue bedroom and laying me on the bed, covering me with his body.

We line up perfectly, his cock nestled in the gap between my thighs and I have to look up just a bit for our mouths to touch.

"Angel." He grabs my chin between his thumb and forefinger. "There are consequences for *everyone* who put you in danger."

"Oh?" That thrill down my spine has nothing to do with the adrenaline of what just happened and everything to do with the dark promise in Sebastian's stormy eyes.

"You deserve a thorough spanking for risking the love of my life like that."

"I'll have to take it, then, won't I?" And my smile is naughty. I want everything from Sebastian. The pleasure and the pain, whatever he gives me I'll ask for more.

This. Him and me. It's a messy sort of family, but it's real. He's the one constant in my life. My north star that I couldn't see because the clouds covered him. But he was always there, shining over me. And now he's *mine*.

"Think you can?" He sucks my bottom lip into his mouth and drags up the hem of my dress. I wriggle to give him access and reach one hand for his hair, tangling and grabbing, and the other for his belt. He wants inside me, and I will give him everything.

"Every day," I promise, and he growls in satisfaction.

EPILOGUE
SEBASTIAN

5 YEARS LATER

I rake my hand through my hair in frustration. "We do this deal now, and my way, or we do not do it at all."

"No." She pouts and crosses her arms. Wearing a little blue skirt and a hairband, you'd think she was in a power suit for all the ground she's giving.

"No to my deal? Or no to now?"

"No." She nods as though that is a reasonable answer.

"Alright. That's it. You forfeit, I get aalllll the chocolate, and you get tickled." I scoop Kelsie up into my arms and tickle her underarms until she wriggles and giggles and shouts delightedly.

"No more tickle, Daddy!"

Our tiny daughter is the fiercest negotiator I know. She's learned from her mother. I stop tickling her and she squirms and cuddles into my chest. Then three seconds later, she bats my bicep with her little fist. "More tickle."

"You are a tyrant," I grumble, but I tickle her as she

requests and Jeanette walks in to find Kelsie hanging backwards out of my arms, flailing and laughing.

"You two," she says with affectionate exasperation. "Weren't you supposed to be making lunch?"

"There was a slight hiccup," I say as I move to lean to the side and kiss my wife. "Did you deal with the problem?"

"Absolutely." Jeanette's eyes twinkle. You'd think that having married a mafia boss at twenty-one she would have been a tempering influence on me. And admittedly, most of our income is from our legal businesses now.

But Jeanette has a core of steel. When we discuss how to proceed with a difficult person, she isn't as ruthless as me, but once someone has lost her trust, she'll tell me to do my worst. She says it's the libra of her sun sign. She balances the evidence, then she comes down hard on the side she thinks is right.

And me? I rarely overrule my wife. She's smart, and kinder than me. I wouldn't give as many second chances as she does, but I do, because she wishes it.

The kiss that was supposed to be brief lingers on until Kelsie complains, "Daddy!" and I have to break away to put her back on her feet.

"Later," I mouth to Jeanette above our daughter's head.

"When the stars are out," she whispers back.

"What are you talking about?" Kelsie demands.

"It's going to be a clear night, and Mummy and Daddy are going to watch the stars together when you're asleep in bed," Jeanette says innocently. "Remember I said you were born under the star constellation of Aquarius? Well that means you should like soup for lunch..." And she has distracted Kelsie, only looking back to me to give me a slow, naughty smile.

Tonight. Under the stars. I'll have Jeanette as I do every

night. But it's special when we can find the time to go up to the glass-roofed sitting room at the top of the house. We still have the flat in London, but most of the time this family home in Berkshire is more practical. And the view from the top is quite spectacular on a clear night.

To be honest, it's even more spectacular to me on a cloudy night when Jeanette will let me leave a light on and look into her violet eyes as I take her. As she rides me. As she comes on my cock for the thousandth time.

Bad as I am, I really don't deserve to be this lucky. But I'll take it all.

EXTENDED EPILOGUE
JEANETTE

5 YEARS LATER, THAT EVENING

I wait with bated breath in the rooftop solarium. The temperature has dropped with the clear night, but it's still warm, and my tiny negligee is sufficient. It's a new one in white silk and lace—the style I know makes Sebastian's cock even stiffer than usual. He can't resist me looking all sweet and pretty and innocent, even when the item in question is only long enough to skim my butt at the back and gapes at the front to reveal my nipples.

The lights are off, and there's just moonlight spilling in from outside, coating the plants, thick rug, and big squashy sofa we have up here with silver. Just the edges, like my husband's hair. He has more silver in his hair now than when we married, but I don't care. It's part of him and makes him all the sexier to me.

Sensation skitters down my back.

He's watching me. I always know.

But I keep my eyes trained on the dark horizon, leaning casually on the waist-height bench that runs along one side of the solarium. It makes my butt stick out a little. The negligee is so short, I bet he can see my pussy lips. This will drive him wild.

The thought is already making me ludicrously wet. I'm aching and needy—weeping for his attention. But there's fun to be had before he fixes it for me.

My breathing is shallow.

Waiting. Waiting.

I wiggle my hips, trying to get a tiny bit of friction to my clit. Not too much. But he's dragging this moment out to make it sweeter. Drawing me into the tension of being just a little nervous about what he'll do.

Will he grab my wrist, for old times' sake? Maybe he'll put me in a choke hold, or pin my arms to my stomach and make me break free? I don't even know if he'll be still in his suit, crisp and controlled, or naked and ready for me. The same game we play, but it's different every time.

But I know he's there, behind me, somewhere.

I think I catch a hint of his blue-wave scent and I start to turn as his arms band tight around my waist, jerking me into his chest and leaving all the air in my lungs behind.

For a second all I want to do is melt into him. His cock is rock solid in the small of my back and I desperately want it inside me. But that's not us. I twist and elbow his side, landing a hit which makes him grunt and the next thing I know, his breath then his mouth is on my neck and he's biting me, hard. I squeal in shock and his tongue laps over the hurt spot, soothing before he sucks.

"That will mark!" I hiss.

His low chuckle vibrates through me. "I know."

I go to kick him, but he steps away easily, lifting me off my feet. I thrash, careful not to actually get too close to hurting him of course, and "accidentally" brush myself against his cock. He spins us around, pressing against my back all the time.

"Let me go." I writhe, trying to slip in his grasp enough to get my nipple to rub on his arm.

"No. You're *mine*." He retaliates by lowering me to that soft rug and covering me with his body, pressing his weight and strength into me and crushing my breasts against the floor. And damn but it's so good. Delicious.

The rug caresses my belly as I wriggle, trying to get more friction. My husband's chest is all smooth and heated skin with the prickle of his hair. As he presses his mouth to my nape, he's rough stubble and wet lips. I try to drag myself away and out from underneath him with my hands. But as I intend, he settles his weight more solidly onto my hips, pinning me. His cock is between my legs and I ease them further apart so the head notches at my soaking entrance. I'm excessively wet for him. Desperate. As he grabs one hand and clasps it hard down on the rug, I reach behind me, gripping at his hair.

"I'm not yours unless you take me." I clench my fist and he grunts at the spike of pain as the silky strands pull tight. "Show me who I belong to."

A growl is all the warning I get before he rears back and then plunges into me. The force shoves me forwards and my cry is part surprise, part relief. There's a smidgen of discomfort too, as he's big, and my body has to stretch out to accommodate him every time. That first entry always has a burn that smoulders into the best fullness. Like I'm stuffed with him.

"Tight, you're so fucking tight, angel," he rasps and I push my hips back to take him more.

He doesn't hold back. As soon as he hits the top of my passage, he's thrusting, one hand still trapping mine, the other on my hip, holding me in place hard enough to hurt. Hard enough to bruise.

I hope I have bruises tomorrow.

Sebastian is always so sweetly conflicted when I admire where his fingers dug in enough to leave his mark on me. He can't bear to have me in pain for any reason, but it makes him hot to see me wear such an obvious sign of possession, and remember how those shadows were pressed into my skin.

Makes me hot too.

"My wife," he snarls as he fucks me. That possessive sends a thrill down my back that's in addition to our violent little game. I'm his, and him overwhelming me like this proves it time after time.

My hand is still in his hair, but I'm not fighting him anymore. I can't. The pleasure of him working in and out of me is too much. Too good. It's all I can do to hang on— barely—to the floor, to him, and to my sanity, as his thrusts rub my nipples onto the softness of the rug, his cock pistons, and then, of course, he reaches around. Releasing my hand, he unerringly finds my clit and strokes.

I'm so primed by our game and the rhythm of his cock, I snap immediately. The pleasure floods me, makes me bone-less and quivering and Sebastian swears, the sound muffled by my hair, but doesn't stop.

Bastard. He doesn't let up thrusting into my passage or circling my clit.

"You're so wet, my beautiful, slutty wife," he says into my ear, but I can hear the tension in his voice, even through the blur of pleasure pulsing through me all the way to my toes. He's breaking too. "You came for me so easily. Did you want your husband's cock?"

"Yes!" The confession is torn from me as my orgasm

eases only as far as he allows it. The pleasure is building again immediately. "I wanted you to take me."

"Good girl," he purrs, and ups his pace, pounding into me mercilessly. "You take my cock perfectly, my good girl."

Those words. That approval from him lights me up again.

"I want you to own me," I pant. He's swelling further against my pussy walls. Close.

"I do. You can feel it, can't you? As I claim what's mine."

"Fill me up. Fuck a baby into me, Sebastian." I'm sobbing now, my body his toy to use. Pliant and yet needy. He's so heavy on me, hard inside me. The uncompromising demand of his cock thrusting and his fingers rubbing pushes me higher and higher.

I twist my head, desperate to catch a glimpse of him. My husband. And he knows. His lips find mine in a kiss that's impossibly soft and tender compared to the harsh slap of our flesh together.

"Come, Jeanette," he demands and because I'm his creature, I crack again, pleasure rolling over me as he pounds me into the floor and kisses me gently.

"I love you," I whisper as my orgasm ebbs away leaving me replete.

And I think that's what tips him over because he roars as he comes, wet heat spilling into and out of me, overflowing. He collapses onto his elbows, keeping some of his weight off me so I'm not totally squashed. Just pleasantly trapped and held.

The shudders that go through him seem almost painful, but I know that they're good, the best, from murmured conversations with my cheek nestled on his chest on so many nights. Sharing secrets and explaining anything and everything that's on our minds.

As both our climaxes recede, Sebastian rolls onto his back and brings me with him to lie tucked into his side.

"I'll never tire of that game," I say into his skin. Another truth. They're too easy with my husband.

"I'll never tire of showing you how much I want and love you, angel."

And that's it. He wants me beyond reason. And he's mine.

THANKS

Thank you for reading, I hope you enjoyed it.

Want to read a little more Happily Ever After? Click to get exclusive epilogues and free stories! or head to Evie-RoseAuthor.com

If you have a moment, I'd really appreciate a review wherever you like to talk about books. Reviews, however brief, help readers find stories they'll love.

Love to get the news first? Follow me on your favoured social media platform - I love to chat to readers and you get all the latest.

If the newsletter is too much like commitment, I recommend following me on BookBub, where you'll just get new release notifications and deals.

amazon.com/author/evierose

bookbub.com/authors/evie-rose

instagram.com/evieroseauthor

tiktok.com/@EvieRoseAuthor

Made in the USA
Columbia, SC
19 December 2024